SINK OR BURN

CRISTY ROAD CARRERA

For all inquiries and usage requests, please contact rights@rowhousepublishing.com or write to Row House Publishing, PO Box 210, New Egypt, NJ 08533.

ISBN: 9781967182039 (Paperback)
ISBN: 9781967182046 (eBook)

Printed in the United States
Distributed by Simon & Schuster

Library of Congress Cataloging-in-Publication data available upon request.

Edited by V. Ruiz
Illustrations by Cristy Road Carerra
Design by Paul Baillie-Lane (www.ingenious-books.com)

First Edition

10 9 8 7 6 5 4 3 2 1

For every untold story of liberation, love, & rock 'n' roll
destroyed by colonization and war.

CONTENTS

PART 1: WELCOME TO PURGATORY

PART 2: JOURNEY TO THE END OF EAST DYSTOPIA

PART 3: A LOVE SONG

PART 1
WELCOME TO PURGATORY

UNREAL

We applied our appliqué, our eyelashes, and our armor: spikes, studs, coiffed bangs, fluorescent chiffons, and bold, striped Balenciaga blouses, all of which had been liberated from a shattered Park Avenue. We were Cheap Glitter, and we looted prime *accessorah*.

Back home in East Dystopia, otherwise known as Old New York, there were no wildfires, and there was no musky embrace of gardenias and shrapnel. The east was dull like smokestacks and concrete; what once had been resorts and faulty empires had now turned into debris.

West Dystopia, the place once called California—what was now Kali Forno to us—was settling into its own detrimental state of post-war fumes. In the inland of Kali, we needed gas masks to breathe and titanium shields for ash season. To arrive safely at tonight's show, we needed spikes and hydraulics on our Astra III so we could drive across Kali's range to the Ohlone coast, where breathing was free.

“I don’t know who I want to be today . . . I guess I just want to be hot.”

“Yeah . . . let’s be hot.”

“Ok. I’ll just be hot.” I stood up, stooping beneath the 12V TV that hung from the ceiling, and assembled a green, shimmering chiffon skirt around my waist. “And tired.”

“Fuck, yeah.” The van shook on a wide right turn, and Fulanito faced his compact, applying his eyeliner in a delicate brokenness that forced me to make great art. “Hot and tired.”

Fulanito was hot and tired and obscured behind all his grieving, but beneath the sheer tulle swath of standoffishness, he was divine and pained. Fulanito wallowed in his dignity and paid no mind to the red tape that stood between his legacy and this moment. Traversing West Dystopia in our green and gold Astra III, we glimmered with purpose.

On the waterfronts of Ohlone, Kali, life had resumed. Reconstructed urban landscapes, wild farms, large installations of protest art, and decriminalized red-light districts all sat on the peaks of the surviving islands’ seaside cliffs.

Exiting Old 880, we were greeted by the pink and red fog that soiled our lungs but looked beautiful in retrospect. Through glimmering embers and disintegrated fog, we reached our destination.

Most of the underground shows in North Ohlone happened in the carcass of the Jack London Inn. The Jack was an abandoned twentieth-century hotel set and sat on the Oakland Bay facing the twinkling noise pollution of rusty, old, and lawless Alameda.

We entered the scene with decadently painted wide eyes and naivete because, just like yesterday, *this* was going to be the best night of our lives.

In the basement, the backstage lounge was raging, so I cowered in a corner of the salty, empty hallway with Fulanito. Everyone looked gorgeous or angry or both, and I was proud to herald their filthy prehistoric battle cry.

However, I could feel the sneering, the discomfort of the onlookers, the media, and the admirers who had built an imaginary framework of who we, *their faves,* were in practice—not a couple, but available queer sluts; you know, like our 2119 promo shot with the double-sided dicks?

I, unfortunately, needed to start accepting the moments that felt divine: this heart, this tour, this fervor spiking the dawn of a squatters' revolution unheard of in my mother's America. I needed to accept the moments that felt intimately cosmic—or rather moments that felt unreal, unclear, and unsafe—because, after all, we didn't have the luxury of time anymore.

That night, I felt fake. I felt brash and bubbly.

"¡Oye! Viva la Revolución!" I greeted old friends in a buzzing, rare confidence as they passed by. I turned back toward Fulanito to catch him staring—at *me*.

He stood against the wall in his midsized glory and with his doe eyes, glossed lips, and heavy black liner, creating a serene middle ground between pain and fashion. Fulanito and I were polarizing and icy as front people. One day, we were the life, the sex, and the show of the party. The next, we were stoic and mean and not popular but infamous, like cold shoulders on warm nights.

He pulled me toward his corner.

"You know, if it wasn't for you, I would have quit this a long time ago." Fulanito whispered the words into my ear, and on the ethereal plane, I fell flat. Here on Earth, I smiled, maintaining a coy, elusive posture.

Fulanito was born and raised in Kali. Ganache, our booking agent and roadie, and I had routed this tour with the intention of bringing Fulanito home for a night, something that could not have happened otherwise, as cross-country travel and the flight industry had become gated by the gatekeepers.

I grabbed his arm, feeling the stiff pinstripe fabric of some high-end blazer—probably vintage YSL or something. "What do you mean?"

Fulanito smiled. His amusement was always paired with a bashful, uncomfortable smirk. I did not know if it was performative or if he was carrying the last bit of innocence left in the Dystopia.

"Hey, come out to the balcony with me," Fulanito commanded, and I followed in tow. We exited the basement, leaving behind the sneering, the staring, and the smell of dried cumin and chlorine that had wafted in from a distressed boutique resort sitting on the Ohlone waterfront like a monolith. This balcony overlooking the fires of his home, his legacy, and my escape was now the first place we'd ever snuck away to.

"So, what do ya wanna tell me?" He looked into my eyes for half a second as we were removed from the common plane of existence. Now, we were in what felt like heaven.

"There's *so* much I want to tell you . . ." Or was it purgatory?

Fulanito was unavailable—newly single and somewhere between grieving and healing. Tonight, we would not kiss.

"C'mere," Fulanito whispered, and I wrapped my arms around his shoulders, clutching his neck with my left hand and knowing I had been here before—throughout lifetimes, continents, and homes. "Breathe with me . . ."

Synchronized into the uncanny rhythm of our hearts and our lungs, we transformed our ruins into paradise, into time-controlled chaos, into chaotic bliss.

My heart did not palpitate—I was home. Our despair waned in tandem with every other breath, and our souls combined into an unflinching cadence of naive hope. We were finally fixed—in time, in space, in unnerving vulnerability.

Fulanito's breath was soft and dangerous at the same time, like love

and femininity. My breath was shy and thunderstruck, like an orgasm.

Fulanito let go and mumbled beneath his collar, "I don't want to stop." He turned away toward the bay.

"What did you say?" I grabbed his arm, he grabbed my body, and we settled back into our breath, our warm embrace a palpable remedy against self-loathing in times of apocalypse.

I wasn't used to equilibrium—it was an awkward four-letter word that waged a war against the flux we called *normalcy.* Dystopia was not balanced, nor sound. I had never really known the peace of the 2050 Post-American Bloom: when blue whales sang and purple mountains sprang from the sparkling Atlantic to the sprawling Pacific. North America was then protected by the Collective's billion-dollar contracts against fracking, dredging, displacement, and genocide; when colonizers hid on the moon and humanity was forsaken.

I was born forty years too late and had to grow up during the Early Desperation Period—when you could choose to be free only by living in metropolitan coastal regions and college towns—knowing that the great divide had already begun to cast shadows over demographics and diasporas who had only recently reclaimed their lands and cultures from seven hundred years of systemic erasure.

In that moment with Fulanito, I was free—free from cultural genocide, from AI terrorism, from the shitty payout in Seattle, and from wanting to be worshiped by whoever was working *that* shift, the one after every show, in every town, where everybody on it knew my name yet none of them could understand how I could be *so sad,* because gosh darn it, I was *so cool.*

This stellar plane of suspended bliss smelled less like lonely nights of warfare and more like the sweat on Fulanito's jawline, dense like live oak with subtle notes of gin and rare earth. For once, I was anchored. My mortal bones froze while my breath vacillated in the iridescent threshold between all the places I've called home and every galaxy I will never know.

This moment was the cataclysm I longed for: the end, the beginning, the abyss—the dismal shuffle—hell, high water, and the aromatic florals in between.

Here, on this balcony, began the unending tension that would send Fulanito and I to the glorious pits of a burning inferno where our naked flesh would finally meet—or to some other kind of hell, some kind of heaven, or some kind of interrogation with the spirits of my ancestors.

Was this even allowed?

Up here in suspension, in this rarely achievable state of being, our hearts and our teeth were in flight, and the ifs, buts, and where's of who brought us here and what happens tomorrow did not matter. Unaffected by the wildfires, the awkward conversations, and the hollow goodbyes, we swung back and forth on some kind of thrill ride.

Up here in suspension, we took a break from everything—for what seemed like the first time.

Back in 2050, when democratic socialism was introduced to the Post-American Bloom's infrastructure, the fascists either disintegrated into their private lives or colonized the moon. By 2073, the moon retaliated, as the Earth has, albeit through harsh climates and psychic attacks to their otherwise secure dispositions. Some made it back to Earth, and thus initiated years of violent upheaval, in attempts to overthrow the Post-American Bloom.

When the Great American Party was founded in 2079, my mother's generation assumed it was a government prank—like, how the fuck could these clowns in vintage Brioni suits and bumblebee-colored vicuña trouser socks overthrow the mass decolonization movement of North America? By 2085, my parents had already given birth to me, signaling a sense of hope. Our world was in tact then—our universal healthcare, our free education, and our sustainable housing—allowing me to come of age with a foolish flare for believing in revolution.

By 2101, the Great American Party had taken control of most of North America—and as it now continued to win in favor of environmental destruction and mass displacements, Fulanito and I stood still. Avoiding the ruckus of our wildest night of tour from our well-concealed overlook, we held each other for first time.

Lost in an indefinite clasp, we tied generations of loose ends.

Up here in suspension, the air was no longer chlorine bleach. It was his lion's breath and my whiskey teeth—burning Monterey pine, live oak ash, fresh-cut grass, and sulfur—dancing beneath the far reaches of West Dystopia and this dilapidated room that had once housed tourists but now housed unrest.

With every exhale, I released my fear of loving someone so deeply that it would become yet another fragile liability in the grand scheme of a looming apocalypse.

Who even was I but a lowly, soft butch who was disguised as a femme in a lime-colored chiffon dress and a full face of makeup and who was escaping my grieving process through drugs and alcohol? *Did I even deserve this moment of self-serving embodiment?*

I looked into Fulanito's eyes and accepted the unnerving truth that this curse may be reciprocated in some lifetime, if not this one. Well, *fuck*, there's no turning back now.

"Hey, fuckers!" Ganache interjected. "Five minutes till showtime!"

"Oh hey, man . . . yeah, totally." Fulanito, doe-eyed and deadpan, scratched his head, trying so hard to care.

"Oh yeah, shit, the show," I said, stumbling over my words.

"Fuckers," Ganache mumbled.

DYSTOPIA

I attempted to shake off the five minutes in heaven that had caressed a lifetime of longing. I faced Fulanito, but he faced forward in a blank, dedicated stare, eyebrows arched toward the sky and eyes wide with determination. We followed Ganache toward the curtains.

The walls of the Jack were covered in twenty years of flyers that had kept the scene loud and proud. Everything smelled like beer specials, old swimming pools, and unsealed bags of bold, musky cumin—a cosmic warming blend of the organic grocery store with no ventilation and the basement punk show.

The Jack was a vast sanctuary to activist and artist communities who had been displaced after the destruction of so many hundred-year-old institutions—the Ella Baker, the PARC, 924 Gilman St., the Long Haul, the Peace Center. These sanctuaries had survived everything until New America.

The lobby was clean and intact, sweltering with floral essences that were lush reminders of regeneration and accessibility. The second floor was where we went to feel important as somewhat depressed songwriters with very little standing sanctuaries in our name. The Jack was a renowned venue for performers in favor of the dissent, from punk rock to jazz to house music to atmospheric monologues in fogs of dry ice.

The greenroom was abundant with complimentary indica cigarillos, Band-Aids, condoms and contraceptives, granola, hummus, yogurt, assorted corncobs made from seven different kinds of corn grown on the land, pitted prunes, cashew mascarpone, and cases of home brew flavored with an array of tropical fruits.

We made it—in whatever sense one could choose to embrace such a rabid notion, as the world was practically in flames. But being known for some years now, we were used to it, and we were grateful.

Our rider always specified the same concoction of chronic gut health supplements, corn-related snacks, anti-anxiety notes, yogurt, ibuprofen, and fruit-infused beverages. These gifts only felt blessed and without unsuspected guilt when we used them to *maybe* save the world.

Tonight's show was a benefit for the Coalition Against Global Fracking.

"Wow, ten thousand, y'all!" Oracle read the fine print on our contracts.

"What! Holy crap." I was not sure how to process that.

"Carajo!" Fulanito paused in a sacred moment of face yoga as he faced the check. "Is that for us?"

"Wow. Can you imagine if we actually had a reason to use this? For, like, nice furniture and stuff?" Reggy was pleasantly cynical.

After all, we didn't spend money on much in Dystopia. Coastal dystopias were one category of New America's Disposable Zoning Regions, where we did not pay rent—not because the Regime had a conscience but because dystopia was ungovernable. Disposable Zoning constantly needed to be nurtured and rehabilitated to thrive, but it was not; thus, the Dystopia received its name. Dystopias were continually devastated by industrial progress, wildfires, erosion, and natural disasters, but they were held by scientists, healthcare workers, contractors, carpenters, social justice initiatives, and food justice programs. A symbiotic relationship with the planet had been enforced when we were kids, before the New American Regime, so some things had just stuck.

In Dystopia, individual committees who had fought on the dissent during the 2111 riots managed our resources. Dystopians paid for electricity and otherwise made their mark. Creatives and healers created joy, aesthetics, embodiment, and safety in exchange for education, public safety, and wellness. Drivers, carpenters, cooks, housekeepers, athletes, educators, mediators, martial arts, self-defense—everyone and everything was *essential*. Dystopia was complex; it was not simple; it was occasionally despairing and violent and in need of affinity and mutual aid in our inner circles; but it was modern survival under a decade of far-right corruption and collective resistance; and occasionally, it was gorgeous.

After fifteen years of New America, I was now at my heart-space again, that awakening that happens when you are healed, or in love, or so traumatized that your wound is your weapon. Although undoubtedly anew, I was still gnawing at the loneliness that I feverishly attempted to entwine with my *allegedly* revolutionary work as a *renowned recording artist*.

Blah.

"Holy crap. I have never been in the same room as a full ten thousand dollars!" I squealed. "I might've just shit myself."

"Let it out, gurl . . ." Fulanito stared at the contract with no words but a subtle smile that only said *I'm finally free.* Every band Fulanito had ever started since his adolescence—Stellar Vomit, Total Waste, Dead Inside—had flourished and then disintegrated at the sight of their own success. Beloved and influential and before their time, all had been fronted or backed by Fulanito's words of heartfelt despair.

This was it, the trajectory he deserved.

I personally never gave a rat's ass about being famous. Sure, I wanted the power to destroy the New American Regime—and I wanted other lost freaks to love my art and sing along when faced with it because that is just the kind and sensitive thing to do; but once that's over, then what? I knew my role was to heal, to create, to infuse joy and truth into defunct platforms that deserve to scream. Fulanito had a similar role, albeit with a greater interest in stability that kept Cheap Glitter warm at night.

Andy the stagehand peeked his head through the curtain. "Heyo! One minute!"

I walked toward my post, instruments in hand, and prepared for a battle between rage and celebration. Singing each song was an organic second nature, thinking about nothing and everything at once.

Home was now *dystopia* because the global hope that had raised us was now dead. And I—still freshly traumatized from the sinking of my home state of Florida—was equally dead inside.

New America had both co-opted and dismantled a former reign of compassion that we had rioted for. New America loved justice and hated poor people. New America loved clean eating and hated sick

the Last

people. New America was old America: minimal and compartmentalized, tired and racist—but *healthy*; it was old America embodied in a gender compliant with society's expectations, enrolled in a state-sanctioned spin class, aware of what is in our food, aware of harm reduction and de-escalation tactics, aware of self, but self-determined—so self-determined that we are not encouraged to love our neighbor, but to be *the prettiest*. New America built a new constitution with a vague creed on justice and liberation executed as laws against cultural, neurological, and physical diversity.

New America was transparent in its creed—the strongest, the fittest, and the most sustainable supremacy was not a marketing scheme but government praxis. Yet New America's policy on liberation—destroying generations of work that healers and abolitionists had fought for at the turn of the century—was clandestine at most.

Sure, there were still purple mountain majesties—fighting for their lives against fracking and displacement. And yes, the ocean was still blue—when it reflected the few clear parts of the sky. Environmental warfare was state facsism's oldest sidekick, and while policy mitigated any resonance of a just society, the Earth choked.

With the sky always shifting between shades of teal, aqua, and taupe, holding onto those priceless moments of aqua and sun-washed teal became haphazard routine.

At least I had Cheap Glitter for yelling my truth into an ether that needed another source of enlightenment. Thanks to the unending Clause P747—an initiative to preserve free speech and pretty much make the Regime look good on a global scale—abolitionist movements were sought after by the Regime despite their impact on reform.

The effort was not clean, but the money was still green.

Quite foolishly, I believed in reform.

The potential access to government funding fueled our tour and our resources. Many Dystopians had access to New American currency but little to no use for it unless it went toward patronizing New American resources. Fortune and commercial growth were not like they used to be, and if state indoctrination and risking covert assassination in exchange for submission was the ticket to "clear" skies and genetically modified "health" foods, then I was going to just sit here in my reactionary bitch pants and eat my permaculturea curds and berries that I grew in my goddamn bathtub.

I was safe here in my makeshift van resembling the postwar love child of a vintage Astro and an ugly Tesla, pouting about the resilience that was impossible to find as a single girl pushing forty.

I didn't even *want* a functional economy.

I wanted a person.

I wanted to be held and validated and looked at in a way that made me wet and confused. I wanted a room to sit in once the music stopped, somewhere I could expect the kind of love that I had only heard of through my Mamá's chismes and my Abuelas' hearsay.

Our last song was our anthem, "Dichosa Traya," a song named after those fucking bad kids who stir the pot and shift history; in ancient Miami lexicon; about transforming self-hate into self-righteousness. The gang vocals and spirited highs flooded the airways and soon dissipated. Amid the silence after the last note, the faulty fuse on an overhead Fresnel blew out, spritzing electric glitter into the dense atmosphere.

WHEN WE WERE YOUNG

Punk rock had died and come back to life so many times in the last one hundred and fifty years that I had to stop pathologizing and accept that it was nothing but a cult—not a dangerous cult, as we lacked a governing body, but a secret club of cool kids who hated themselves and had little agency over their coolness. We were living in a very specific way and listening to very specific artists and receiving a very specific historical context of music in a very specific way—thus, we could smell the wrong side of history permeating the racist, misogynist spectacle of New American modern rock. The sanctity of the sound that represents our region or ethos, our *scene,* is often what kept us alive at one point or another. It's what set our foundation on how we engage with gratitude, growth, success, wealth, class war, how we treat people, and how we treat ourselves.

Punk's sometimes dogmatic and sometimes revolutionary ideals informed our weird jobs, our weird bikes, our homemade shampoos, our discourse on gender, our unapologetic antiracism, and our acceptance of the futile.

Yet, this was the life of so many people on the margins. I was always so angry that Punk Rock itself seemed to have co-opted self-sufficiency, let alone *anarchy*—a political system hundreds of years older than punk rock.

Why was it sO pUnK RoCk to be resilient? To be poor? To piss on the sidewalk? As if punk rock had trailblazed oppression? Why couldn't punk rock stay angry, anarchist, antiracist, feminist, or class-conscious—or its whole other brand of shocking—while also staying aware of its role in revolution? Aware of its exclusivity? Its weirdness and circus-like configuration? Its history that reads like bible study and its nonstop display of noise that may alienate *some*? Its difficult take on cleanliness and its ultra embrace of survival—to the point that we romanticize struggle?

I mean, don't get me wrong: this worked for me as a Gemini with heavy Cancer placements. Utopia and nostalgia give me life. And with a midheaven in Pisces, hell knew I wanted love and community and stank potlucks in the woods and more love, again and again, but through art and music because I never considered fiscal stability.

But I wasn't a hippie—*heavens no*—I wanted to throw chairs and puke and yell about shit.

My punk rock was a meat-and-potatoes, it-is-what-it-is, rock 'n' roll bag of dicks. Whether or not it was adjacent to so many people's revolutions, it was still comfortably rotting and fermenting in a heart-wrenching, deeply specific bracket of sound.

Punk rock, the sound, was pure and unlike anything—it's who we were as artists. Punk rock, the community, was familial and unending—it's who we were as people. Punk rock gave us the ability to easily find respite or friendship based on that one sticker on a mailbox or that one patch on a backpack of that one band who'd toured with us the summer of 2099, when we were 18 and not Cheap Glitter, but T.U.R.D.—Totally Unidentified Rectum Dust.

Now we're Cheap Glitter, and I'm still just a weird girl shitting on what's become of my clear skies and bright lights and trying to call East Dystopia home yet still calling it chaos or escape.

Whether punk rock played a savior or not, every moment I spent away from home, I felt my bones crack and my guts cackle. I felt calcium deficiency, acid reflux, and sexual repression entangle themselves in my sacral chakra. But touring was necessary to spread gospel, to exceed boundaries, and to fortify our relationships to that chaos of home.

We were New Yorkers no matter where we slept. We were wide-eyed and hopeful about our storefronts and our art. We were still the bodega next to the corner bar, next to the mosque, next to the temple, next to the church and the steeple and the displaced people. We were the roti shop and the punk club and the vintage shop lining cracked cobblestones and broken dreams. We were sparkling histories of Busby Berkeley crosswalks, casual flash mobs, electric marquees, and electric fireflies asking you to *buy buy buy* even though all you wanted to do was sit back with a hot dog or a slice and kiss someone under those lights like you meant it.

At the end of the Post-American Bloom, New Yorkers just seemed hungry to *buy buy buy* things like modern fashions by gay Black downtown designers, rare algae butters, and tickets to musicals about destroying the looming regime. Since healthcare and education were free for all and since housing and organic fruits and vegetables were affordable and accessible as long as we were eligible or at least offered a community service, we could splurge on life when life allowed us.

Now we just splurged on purpose, taking a journey that was neither pleasure nor work but a religious pilgrimage against the destruction of our land. And while there was no freedom to conquer and destroy, there was the room to write and yell about it.

Cheap Glitter was our echo chamber.

I'd started the band with my old friends, Oracle and Reggy. I sang and played guitar, Oracle played drums, and Reggy played bass. Eventually, Fulanito joined—he played saxophone—and we all sang together. I wrote most of the songs about my love traumas, cultural assimilation, and my crush. Fulanito also wrote some songs about displacement, grieving, and his crush.

I had been writing songs pretty much since I was born. It had started as a way to celebrate the beauty of nothingness—my first song was called Tetas de Mantequilla—which I wrote about a Victorian doll that, to me, looked like a stick of butter. I wanted to celebrate the mysticism of my favorite anatomical taboo that I had yet to understand—*tits*—in an ode to my favorite doll. My songwriting eventually evolved into the general storytelling of an overactive mind and into a profound desire to make my heartstrings articulate and universal—therefore, I would never have to explain how I felt to anyone, ever. Alas, twenty-some years passed, and people wanted to listen. So, I decided to keep performing until they couldn't take it anymore.

We had done alright as a band, thriving during collapse, and maintaining the momentum that had kept us going in the beginning. It was a reward, a blessing—and now I had no idea how I would ever navigate the disproportionate space between grieving and gratitude.

We packed up the van and bid farewell to the Jack and the wildly unexpected boost in morale. We'd needed this, as our next stop was

the New American township of Trust, which meant evading active wildfires from Baja to old Dallas and, for the first time, entering the BioDome—the Regime.

Facing the deterioration from the passenger window, I always forgave our hearts at night. State and media have a way of turning sacred geniuses into infantilized, objectified cartoon characters, complicating an individual's connection to self.

When we were young, we chose drugs to remove the facade in order to stay human while we sang and danced and did the gods' work. We chose healing or sobriety when our trajectories made us feel worthy—so we gave back and found wholeness. The ability to continue giving back to ourselves and to those we love now depends on our sense of grounding. If the industry is powerful enough, it will take that away so we can beg and suffer at the mercy of our purpose. And if we find that peace and grounding again despite the odds, we will then fear our safety, our security, our COINTELPROs, our Mark David Chapmans, and our worst selves. This was the minefield of fame, of art, of rock 'n' roll—and so, another world is possible in the loneliness of tour, in the 3-a.m. pep talks with your band, and in the warm embrace of your torrid love.

Fulanito was sitting on the other end of the backseat bench. He looked over and said nothing, but I felt everything.

That day, I could not understand the fear that had once swelled when I'd signed the contract to perform in Trust. I was reeling from feeling too hard, and it felt like drugs. The rarity of my confidence sat in my arteries and in my spine, all left behind by self-made profit and Fulanito's embrace.

Fulanito was the offspring of Peruvian and Italian carpenters, musicians, and farmers. He had been raised around a rare atonement to nature that heightened his organic curiosity and challenged his submission to the music industry's plastic lining. His roughneck bones and inherited knowledge of growing things like chrysanthemums and orchids made him a better rockstar than the rest of us. His mother had resided in West Dystopia, where she'd organized Unitarian-Universalist community and dissent. Her life was taken by what the doctors called lung cancer, and Fulanito called the nuclear holocaust of southern Kali. His father, long separated from him and his mother, and newly reconnected to Fulanito's inner threshold, was now an unsuspected silver lining. Grieving countless family and friends was commonplace in Dystopia, and Fulanito was no stranger to unwarranted catastrophe despite West Dystopia's symbiotic and constructive relationship with nature. Settled in a destabilized peace between seeking security and blazing the trail, Fulanito radiated reckless abandon.

We settled into the back seat, cracking jokes and threatening to open the tinned fish. So commenced an intimate tug-of-war of suspected flirtation, through Morse code and inflections disguised as a morbid ride to Trust.

We had a gig at the LGBTQ Coalition for Rights and Advancement, which sat right at the old Texas–Oklahoma border in New America's BioDome. Once a sanctuary of Navajo leadership and now a ground for Native displacement, the region was disguised as a center for cultural diversity and aptly named Trust.

Yes—we lost community, as our attempts at infiltrating the state reeked of betrayal. Yes, our compas and our elders began questioning our affiliation to the resistance as a band who could bank $10K off a DIY performance through P747 creative grants. The decision to trade in our sanctity for a large sum of money held nuance that was difficult to grasp, but still, we held onto conviction.

Alas, we were the discomfited chosen ones who agreed to trudge across forbidden wastelands and fund our revolution through song, joy, dance, and soul-sucking compromise. We stood beside false revolutions and broken institutions in order to generate wealth and therefore break the system from within.

Well, sometimes attempting to casually generate millions of dollars feels dehumanizing.

"What on earth are you even doing?" was the common response to our agreement to play the Coalition. "Just move to the BioDome and give up, why don'tcha?"

Except we knew exactly what we were doing. We knew we were banking $200K in one night of doing what we love, albeit on pins and needles, to the faux diversity elite. We knew we were harnessing a potential pass into the infrastructure that we could probably omit through strategic, divisive planning. We knew we were entertainment for the suit and ties of diet culture and toxic wellness led by Caitlin Monseratt, an heir of the 2111 Coalition Against Toxic Autonomy—another term for diet fascism and systemic body policing.

However, we were getting our bills paid, our dues paid, and our funds immediately wired to the revolutionary work being done by the 125-year-old institution, the Sylvia Rivera Law Project, to stop the implementation of the Coalition for Rights and Displacements Act in Old New York—an effort to eventually ban squatting in order to tax East Dystopia.

Sitting here in our van, after five hours of driving and a stop on the cusp between New America and West Dystopia, we were too close, and the tepid, dry air had become thick with resent. We were no longer decompressing—no longer living our best lives.

Oracle was perusing the Farmer's Almanac in preparation for surviving the winter after our return to old New York. Oracle was constantly preparing us, as her strength and resilience sat within a crevice in her solar plexus, making it easy to give without question. Her earthbound dyke qualities kept my airy pansexual mess afloat. She was a licensed therapist with two degrees in human socialization. And after leaving behind a career that held structure, Oracle chose to wield her magic through instruments and *smashing shit*.

Oracle's mother passed away during the old regime at an age that had forced her to grow into a warrior long before any of us would have felt capable. By eighteen, Oracle had become a living legend—mullet-hawked, tattooed, enrolled in an exclusive university where the population was 85 percent male, and fronting Heist: the mid-Atlantic's coolest fucking resurgence of turn-of-the century Riot Grrrl sound.

Now, fifteen years later, Oracle ditched the bleached mullet hawk for purple braids that held sacred maps of her complex Trini and southern lineages. Her degrees kept us together, and as both our skins-queen and tour manager, she always ensured we never missed a beat in our songs or internal conflict. We loved and hated her dedication to saving the world, as every so often she could not just pack up and go. Today, we were blessed, as Oracle chose to pack for longer than usual.

Ganache alternated between driving and sleeping. We did not question this. If anything, we were jealous and didn't mind taking the reins behind the wheel in exchange for his otherwise constant availability. Ganache was a loner and a stoner and a lady of leisure, as they would have said in the old world. After being slowly sequestered from the Midwest to either Dystopia, Ganache chose to fuck that—learning harm reduction skills, survival skills, van maintenance, biodiesel management, and weightlifting. Ganache was the underground's roadie superstar, pivoting

KEEP THIS DOOR CLOSED
READY
EAT
2121 FARMER'S ALMANAC
2121 FARMER'S ALMANAC

from one touring indie legend to another and traveling up and down the Dystopias and sometimes even on boats to South America.

Reggy was ready to perform physically—but mentally? It was his turn to dwindle in the paranoia of what's happening to the land and soil of his friends and family.

Reggy was born and raised in upper Appalachia on a mountaintop that was sacred to the Indigenous resistance and land redistribution of 2055. Reggy's family was a mixed concoction of Piqua Shawnee healers and Cherokee farmers. Reggy was celebrated as a Two-Spirit teen by his family and came out as transgender in his early twenties. During the latter years of the Post-American Bloom, the Regime's initiatives swelled, and safe access to healthcare dwindled. Merging his past as an aspiring scientist with his present as a reactionary punk rocker, Reggy felt angry, yet unbothered by the disproportionate shifts in Dystopia's socialized healthcare. Long waits for medications hurt the bulk of Dystopians, but Reggy could practically make colloidal silver out of nuts and berries, so we were not surprised when he extracted oxidative cleavage of the sidechain of cholesterol and turned it into pregnenolone in a glass incubator—a cocktail often referred to as testosterone.

Reggy's ability to create artificial supplements out of elemental compounds was once his purpose as both a healer and an abolitionist. Reggy had never been on a trek to play music: he'd chosen science for money and Indigenous medicine for lifeblood. Oracle and I met him in naturopath therapy—we were both patients.

Around 2115, during the first fall of the resistance, Reggy lost his father and brother during the initial bombing of northern Appalachia, now dubbed Tranquility. This was the rebrand of Appalachia, a patronization of its sacred concepts of peace, freedom from industrialization, and ensuring Indigenous knowledge informs the developing relationship between humans and soil. Tranquility was a false divide between the sovereign Dystopias and New America, and it was not tranquil—it was war-stricken.

As the wealthy conservative classes built personal Earthships all over Appalachia, Reggy eventually felt too depleted for his chosen work. Glassware was now too fragile, and it came time to put his callouses to work. Having plant knowledge and working with the earth were renowned skills, securely passed down to surviving generations of Appalachians. Reggy had now uncovered a new purpose: to scream from the rooftops, the Bio Zones, the forbidden structures, and sacred homes; to play bass guitar and sometimes harmonica in Cheap Glitter; and to feel free, for once.

So, he sat, enraged, pouring over the development of Tranquility, the displacement of his family, and a livestream of *Appalachian Spring.*

What was one to do besides sell out their band for hundreds of thousands of dollars?

Reggy stewed in the polarizing war between being a stalwart, available member of a unit that was once home and a unit that now granted him the license to go the fuck off.

Fulanito was always fucking right off—in the back seat, isolated from the rest of either the band or the world, crooning over whether the Regime will heed his intent. Fulanito was a songwriter before anything else—a creator and a wizard, yet a neurotic parent to his words.

We were about to perform for a room of soul-crushing zombies who worshiped a school of thought fabricated by a Christian scientist android whose message kept poor Jesus rolling in his proper grave, perpendicular to Mecca, and covered in bread, roses, and war-torn Arab ash.

TOG

We fucking hated this crap as much as everyone who questioned our actions. This was *not* the kind of compromise we'd agreed to back in the day when we signed to a major label and garnered the hearts of radicals and norms alike. We'd opened for pop stars and jazz icons then. But now we were no longer punk rockers—we were musicians with a purpose who, every so often, exited their parameters of safety: punk.

Alas, here we were, making sure we showered before we bore our souls to a power-hungry receptacle of filth—the fucking Regime.

New America's BioDome was invisible to a driver or onlooker, as entering New America always involved some kind of detour through a mountainside or some underground tunnels followed by extensive investigation.

Once we exited the Southwest Junction Tunnel, the sky was blue. The grass was green. There were birds. There was an overall silence humming along the oxygen streams that seeped through the cracks in the BioDome. The atmosphere cackled when the wind brushed against a tall oak tree or, sometimes, a buzzing bee, as the simulation of the world we once knew was in an indefinite state of refurbishment. The scents were too fresh, pungently artificial. The paths were paved with tumbled pebbles of precious minerals—tiger's eye, vanadinite, pyrite, and rutilated quartz—once honored for their metaphysical properties, now only decorative paths and placeholders.

We pulled up in the Astra at the entrance to the Coalition. We were greeted by valet bots and an armed guard. Valet parking was mandatory, so we obliged with trepidation.

We walked toward a tall, pink marble structure, ominous and washed out, that had been placed delicately in a field of peonies. A staunch, well-dressed host with a coiffed blonde side swoop and in a casual Armani suit greeted us at the entrance.

"Welcome, Cheap Glitter! I'm Braden, your liaison for the evening. Welcome to New America!" Braden led us through courtyards, gardens, and towering palms. The traction on the ground's surface reminded us that we were not on our soil, but in a showroom of what once had been. Walking through beds of fauna and endangered plants had never felt so violating and ungrounded.

New America's BioDome was a tangible simulation, and frankly, as my abuela would say, I could not.

NEW AMERICA

I wasn't scared to die. I was always grieving something—my family, my youth, the whispers among the drunks after I'd paced from the Romper Room to a slice on Delancey St. and back again. Before they'd shut it down after one hundred and fifty years, the Lower East Side's Romper Room was a good enough reason to keep believing in art as revolutionary praxis. I was silently grieving the unchartered histories of punk rock, soul, hip-hop, disco, drag, and these revolutions that came, went, and festered in the bones of Dystopia.

The pause in technological advancement that happened during the Post-American Bloom had allowed for a regeneration of nature and the spirit. The calm we had been born into came from a collective left—albeit disintegrating at the sight of a thirsty right.

Ever since New America had successfully spread into the waterfronts, sprawling its rampant oil rigs across the land and implementing its deforestation practices, the hole in the ozone layer aggressively expanded. This regression birthed The Disposable Zoning Regions, where erosion, rising sea levels, and highly temperamental UV rays made living conditions subpar for the cushioned elite, yet manageable through knowledge and mutual aid for the wiser and reactionary. After the 2111 riots, Disposable Zones became Dystopia—home.

East Dystopia ran from upper Saskatchewan to my family's once home of Miami—areas largely desecrated through both systemic and environmental disasters. From the east to the west, Dystopia was born out of the Regime's obsession with offshore fracking. Its interest in gutting the land for oil and cobalt was far superior than that of nurturing the multitude of ecological universes that thrived in the post-American bloom. While weaponizing the lexicon of the left, concepts like renewable energy and sustainable farming were violently redefined in New America.

There was so much work to do—and I usually didn't swear our songs would stop New America, but our success felt miraculous and not shy of God's will.

The ebb, flow, and downfall of sustaining a do-it-yourself art practice will be the death of any artist who wants to be famous more than they want to express something that is inside of them that is on fire and unwilling to stay silent. Doing my part was full of hope and passion and demoralizing compromise—this was historical heresy . . . and I could not stop thinking about it as I sat in this exclusive, empty field where touching the soil was theoretically permitted.

We were not surprised—governments have always disguised control and coercion as safety measures—like Homeland Security and Immigration Customs Enforcement, institutions that disintegrated during the Post-American Bloom. The Bloom's initiatives had included Medicare for all, the abolition of prisons as they'd been known, the flourishing of harm reduction culture, transformative justice, economic socialism, the abolition of factory farming, the rise of solar energy, and a public school system that had taught survival rather than assimilation. The Bloom was the America that had broken the elephant's tusk and the donkey's inconsistency.

Before Dystopia, the Post-American Bloom had housed a democratic socialist republic unheard of to both Americans and socialism itself. My mother's rose-tinted America had been heralded by the Collective: a diverse team of abolitionists, social justice movement leaders, and far-left politicians who had grouped together after abolishing the electoral college in 2045, when the American Civil Liberties Union had had the same level of authority as Congress.

Alas, empires destroy everything. During the Bloom, culture, thought, values, and a global stance on social justice rippled through societies and cultures for decades. This was the Earth's waking period after the unbridled decline and genocide of the mid-twenty-first century. Following the 2050 Revolution, endangered species were regenerated, societies made peace pacts, and environmental terrorism waned. I was born into a world where American soil was rematriated to Native stewardship and the Gaza Strip to Palestine. Holistic spirituality blurred the threats of religious denomination, as magic became commonplace. I learned the history of olive trees, pyramids, Allah, Jesus, the Torah and Yorubaland in school, through a world history curriculum that explained spiritual conquest, systemic atrocity, and human resilience. However, the Post-American Bloom only lasted for about forty-five years, until 2099 when Geoff B. Abaddon gained incredible popularity through generational wealth, the quietly thriving right-wing economies who had been nurturing ties to neighboring imperialist regimes, and good ol' American anti-communist propaganda.

The turn of that century felt bleak, idealistic, and foolish. Most people sat on the sidelines or partied, believing in the subtle merge between social democrat values and a conservative regime. We all romanticized the twentieth century, its civil rights movements, and its class and cultural warfare—its wiggle room for self-governance if you were financially stable or feral enough. We all knew that we would continue to scream against and thrive in spite of nations and leaders in order to sustain the rallying cry my generation had been born into.

But New America was so new, so fresh, and so dense with ultimatums.

The first National War against the Post-American Bloom was in 2100, when I had just turned eighteen. After one full year of rioting and a successful guerrilla coup d'etat led by the conservative movements' constituents, Geoff B. Abaddon threatened nuclear war on the Americas, and casualties ensued. This blow to the Western Hemisphere decimated lives and communities. There was no remorse, only celebratory violence.

Geoff B. Abaddon was a violent megalomaniac with idealized notions on how to maintain some sort of American Bloom through coercive manipulation and empty promises of welfare, and New America was his experimental prototype in social and cultural cleansing. Eventually, after years of lecturing, gathering minions, and coercing a nation of immigrants into fleeing his chosen territories or risking nuclear assault, Geoff B. Abaddon was elected president of the United States of America by a reformed electoral college and a right-wing dynasty peddling a modern-wellness pyramid scheme.

Abaddon's hope for a New America was built on fracking—a cash crop. So, they went for the coasts and the Rockies first.

Fracking was heralded as the new economy and became a flourishing job market for communities uninterested in cultivating and

WELCOME
BULLSHI
WHITE NOTIONS
MIND CONTROL
INDOCTRINATION BY ASSIMILATION
THE REBIRTH OF A NATION
THE REBIRTH OF A NATION

working within the fields our then-America had held close: medicine, technology, civil liberties, education, agriculture, and environmental protection.

Fracking is the process of drilling into the earth and using high-pressure fluid to fracture rock and extract the natural gas held within it. After this fluid—a mixture of water, sand, and various chemicals such as methanol, ethylene glycol, and propargyl alcohol—is blasted at high pressure through the well and into the rock, the natural gas begins to seep from the fractured rock and collect in the well—*if we're lucky.* Without extraneous safety regulation and outrageous caution, fracking poisons groundwater, pollutes surface water, destroys natural landscapes, threatens wildlife, and can eventually erase ecosystems and civilizations.

After five years of rash, insatiable, and violent imperialism, hope was canceled, the coasts were diminished, and a once blooming and rehabilitated America was defiled.

Still, as a fourth-generation Latinx-American from a lineage of women who have fled all kinds of fascism, I learned that revolutions can take any form—but not always on the right side of history.

My family was from Florida; we were mostly Cuban with Colombian, Moroccan, and Creole roots and branches—a Global South cocktail that made me a jaded, uncompromising warrior and a very stylish bitch. Florida, once autonomous and lush in tropical vegetation and wildlife, was left to rot under the guise of governmental protection.

After the Legion Pact of 2099, Florida became a commonwealth for the Great American Party before being fully colonized after the elections. Oil rigs filled the borders of a still fragile Everglades County, and millions of Calusa, Miccosukee, and Seminole communities were displaced or destroyed. The disregard of metropolitan centers from Naples to Miami widely dispersed a violent smog of rare minerals, inundating the air with new and uninhibited toxins.

Florida was already fragile, having only just survived the messes left behind during the first half of the twenty-first century; and even when I was a kid and running around the vegetation, the strange animals, and the flowing phosphorescence, Florida had still been fighting hurricanes and sinkholes.

In 2103, one year into Abaddon's presidency, Florida became fracking's hot bed. From Ocala to Big Cypress, oil extractions off the Gulf Coast became abundant, cheap, and unregulated.

On Florida's southeastern coast, we still had our cultures, our epicenters, and our art. The colors of our souls were salmon, aqua, and white, then magenta at dusk, when the clouds became devastatingly fabulous. Florida was a wild woman, holding onto the spells and secrets of priestesses and healers who'd nestled into the sacred Atlantic coasts of Asilio.

Asilio was the name for Florida's lower half—a river of grass surrounded by a beach with no Coast Guard, a horizon with no criminalized dotted line.

During the Post-American Bloom, the Everglades were returned to Miccosukee stewardship, awakening the lush fauna and sacred ecosystems that had suffered through most of the twenty-first century, forging pathways between the swamp and the sea. There had been no embargo against Cuba, no occupied Puerto Rico, and no colonized Haiti. Left-leaning governments were undeterred by the old regimes, and they always were willing to learn or grow or at least be held accountable for both acts of liberation and crimes against humanity. These triumphs kept the citizens loud and resilient.

"Mi Reina" is what I called myself back then—it's what my mom called me, what my abuelas called me, what the punk elder at the newsstand called me when I would stop by asking for Stellar Vomit's cover spreads. I was La Reina, and I was unstoppable; I was young, and I believed in punk and revolution and participating in dissent.

I started to dream of New York City around 2096. This was around the time that Miriam Aba Aye, the alleged founder of the Collective, had passed away in a Seneca Village hospice that'd kept her close to the reinstated yet shrinking Harlem neighborhoods. In Florida, my mom and tías mourned and lit candles and made promises to never let the Bloom's evolution stray. Calm and unbothered, they believed they would be able to overthrow the Great American Party and its looming destruction.

To our shock and our aching dismay, those were some of Florida's final years, as fracking and the new regime had no qualms with mass murder.

Through the early years of the Great American Party's reign, Florida's unregulated fracking industry was a free-for-all for oligarchs and fascist warmongers, and the Regime unabashedly extracted and destroyed the veins, the arteries, and the pulse of the bellowing mangrove gardens and the sacred swamps.

Florida's lungs were in its river of grass, the Everglades. Its tongue was in its panthers, vultures, and toads. Its soul, in its alligators that carved sanctuaries for egrets and salamanders; and its heart, in the coconut trees, the medicinal algae, and Lake Okeechobee. Like in a human, an attack to one of Florida's vital organs was an attack to the wholeness of its mortality.

On a rare occasion in 2110, and in conjunction with eclipses, tornados, full moons, and tropical storms, the Regime initiated a blast of radiation to extract the undesirable properties of the limestone bedrock that held Florida above water. This caused an oil spill off the shores of Naples and a 7.2 magnitude earthquake. Thus, Florida began its uncanny and accelerated descent.

A population of over twenty million people died from toxic air quality and extreme flooding in under a month.

We lost everything.

Nuclear drama was still a hush-money mess, a parlor game, a gamble in the underbelly. Thus, state-sanctioned human rights violations quietly, yet still loudly, killed the last remaining untold stories of my ancestors—my family in their golden 80s and 90s, an era that should have been reserved for beauty and calm.

And I'm unwilling to let that slide.

After thirteen years of transforming irritated, tired skin into armor, I had no idea how the universe could ever rebuild itself after the twenty-first century, after a resilient pandemic and the commodification and desensitization of radical thought, after the genocide against Palestine and the occupation of the Democratic Republic of the Congo.

But it did. In my mother's stories, the people rose up against the greed and environmental terrorism that lasted well into the 2050s. I heard that the war against fascism didn't even harm a civilian—just a decaying infrastructure.

In 2116, Geoff B. Abaddon was assassinated, and an artificial intelligence robot replaced him as president. The empty promises of New American values then commenced—liberal, yet violent, and right-wing, yet soft.

In New America's BioDome, superficial greenhouse farming on dead soil replaced the concept of regenerating forests, and natural ecosystems dwindled throughout an extreme rise in GMO food and medicine. The New American Regime also held a false interest in identity politics—Black lives, queer rights, disability rights, reproductive justice. These were all spoken of and articulated, but only by propagating these radical freedoms in popular media while denying them to the oppressed; such was the broken politics of the turn-of-the-century America that the Great American Party just *loved* to celebrate.

America was, once again, my great grandparents' America—but turned up sideways. Exhausted conservative Post-Democrats were no longer denying the fascist agenda or even pretending to question it. They were celebrating it, as if they could finally breathe.

Through those years, I felt numb. Headlines screamed: a fascist man dies; a fascist robot run by fascist men takes over—same shit, more computers, more social justice buzzwords. Still, the truth made me shake: New America was a world superpower being run by AI, and it was a success story in technology and humanitarian aid despite the body count in its landfills. How had New America become a global model for advancement?

I had no fucking clue and would rather not bat a lash.

Instead, I looked at my hands. Here in the BioDome, I did my nails on this pink tufted chaise lounge overlooking a gorgeous sunset free of smokestacks and neon yellow clouds yet doused in fear and loathing. I digressed here—in the thick of New America, of middle Dystopia.

I sat poised and arched and hoping that Fulanito watched from the other side of the room. He was trying on various boots and shoes donated by the Regime itself while Oracle opened a case of cosmetics and Reggy slicked back his hair with an assortment of shimmering amethyst pomades.

“Should we trust the accoutrements?” Oracle picked up a set of false lashes and inspected their peculiar texture. “Y’all, this could have anthrax . . . just saying.”

“That’s real.” Reggy put down the remainder of the amethyst goop. “Gonna raw dog my hawk tonight.”

Team Cheap Glitter was wise enough to know that copious amounts of cannabinoids or Lexapro or damiana and lemon balm tinctures was the surefire way to perform and perform well.

Tonight would be a riot, albeit not the kind of riot my abuela, Ultima, or Ulta, had once told me about. Ulta’s riot had involved fifty years of the Lower East Side protesting and singing the kinds of songs we liked to write. It had starred drag queens, dancers, magicians, decadent hosts, and an underworld that would keep us creating until death. Ulta’s riot had housed jazz clubs and punk clubs and societal misfits whose storefronts would survive revolution after revolution.

I loved that riot.

HUNGRY EYES

I'll never forget March 2112, when Cheap Glitter had landed on a marquee in Times Square as our cultural autonomy held on by a thread. To be so close to our roots, our predecessors, and some mall pizza—without the red tape or the bureaucracy—had been a celebration of freedom. The sidewalk was a crossover between evening frocks and leather jackets, disgusting shoes and faux furs, bike racks and stiletto pumps, all united for the common cause of antiwar rock 'n' roll. We performed at midnight. Fulanito—who, at the time, I had never spoken to—had stood in the center of the front row, singing along to every song and convulsing to the beat of his liberation.

And so, I never held my breath at the chance of saying that *those were the days* . . . except for the fact that I felt so goddamn worthless and so full of self-loathing, so tortured and inebriated yet so inspired to revel in my community. We had not gone to war; we had not chosen New America. But we did choose to maybe try and manipulate it, to break it a little from the periphery.

The pillars at the Coalition were made of Madagascar vanilla–scented marble, and the walls of sacred quartz lined with decorative strands of onyx. The Coalition struck us like lightning or pangs of the past. We had forgotten the fresh scent of finely preserved architecture, the crisp resonance between concrete and soul. We settled into our routine, despite the undeniable sensation that our world had been taken from us. Looking towards the pillars, I sighed for days gone by. Afterall, ornate columns always took me back to 2112—the year that got away, the year I talked to Fulanito for the first time.

I'd been waltzing, drunk, by myself; and it was dusk in the NYC FiDi on an easy Sunday. Below Victorian towers and twinkling electric windows, I'd just turned a trick that had left me not breathless, but wrecked and ready to retire. I was pushing thirty, sick of pretending to be twenty-one, and eager to massage my elevens—my third eye—with a violent thrust.

"Hungry eyes . . . one look atchu . . . and I can't . . . disgui—ui-ui-uise . . ." I pounced from one Supreme Courthouse pillar to the next, reciting one of my favorite turn-of-the-century lovelorn lyrics by the obscure yet not forgotten: Eric Carmen.

"Yeah, I've got . . . hungry ey-ey-eyes . . ." What could I say? I had an archaic, mammalian flair for feeling deep romantic love.

"I feel the magic between you and I . . . I . . . I . . ." A voice echoed from beyond the courthouse and into the soft temporal region below my depleting, hungry eyes. "Yeah, I've got . . ."

"Hungry eye—eye-eyes . . ." I responded and traced the echo toward an unending fairy tale now ready to transpire. "Now I've got you—in my si-i-i-igts . . . with those . . . hungry eye-eyes . . ."

"Now did I take you . . . by surprise?" The voice was Fulanito. He paused and kept singing while I kept twirling into a rare disposition where the sky was, shockingly, the limit. I could shit on my job. I could pick up my guitar and do whatever I was destined to do. I lived in a country where financial stability required diligence but included an array of decriminalized nightlife options for artisans like me, options that had been set into motion by distressed and jaded millennial financiers with power.

"With my . . . hungry eyes . . ." My spins de-escalated, and I swayed at Fulanito's sobering pace. When Fulanito sang to me, I felt free.

"Now I've got you"—Fulanito pointed at me—"in my sii—iii-ights . . ."

I glanced with an absent stare and sat omnipresent between the lines.

"Hey, wait, don't you sing in Cheap Glitter?" Fulanito recognized me, and then I realized he was that weirdo who'd been fervently journaling on the curb outside the show; the multi-instrumentalist-songwriter-artist formerly of Stellar Vomit, of Dead Inside, and of every band I'd ever cried to; the wing-nut genius who deserved to be known but was too wild and inconsistent in his branding. I realized he was that cute femme guy I'd always wanted to fuck or, at least, talk to.

"Yes, that's me."

This was the beginning of something sickening, of epic proportions, of mind, body, and sound made to sit the fuck down.

When I'd met him, Fulanito had been in a somewhat monogamous relationship with a brilliant and generous butch water sign, and—frankly—anyone under twenty-five felt too young for me, a jaded twenty-eight-year-old at the time. *But,* we needed a saxophone player, and the universe had offered just that.

Nine years had passed, and now Fulanito was single, not ready to mingle, but ready to investigate his sense of self. By this point, I'd become a professional masturbator and a born-again virgin, the world was ending, and the president was a robot. I was NOT surprised that we were here, feeling nostalgic about high-end architecture, like our connections to skyscrapers and courthouses were about sculptural renaissance as artful shelter as opposed to judicial bureaucracy and every time we'd been arrested.

We were all just animals fawning at the clean energy, crystal staircases, and eye-candy facades of the posh, hypocritical New America. High-end structures were still ivory cages; they executed a sort of classical elitism that kept "clean" energy racist and expensive.

"Ten minutes till showtime, fellas!" Braden, our liaison, yelled through the crack in the greenroom's French doors.

"Ugh. I am not your fucking fella, Chad," I mumbled as I applied a mauve lip.

One aspect of New America's diversity plan was to unilaterally simplify gender in language by adapting masculine pronouns as universal signifiers of humans—like old Spanish.

It had been about five years of this abhorrent reconstruction, although it seldom mattered in Dystopia, where our bodies and our identities were autonomous languages of their own. But now we paraded New America for coin, and I'd haphazardly forgotten how much I hated proving or explaining my gender to the elite gender gatekeepers. I identified with terms like *bitch* and *cunt* and *dick* as expletive expressions of my reactionary, inconvenient energy. *Society* wanted me—a musical icon—to present as a precisely non-binary cartoon character who relished in the academic language of postmodern gender theory so that my delicate pairing of feminine accoutrements with an unsuspectingly masculine aura could be easily explained to heterosexuals.

"Well, sorry, Regime cunts, don't fucking talk to me while I'm putting on my lip," I mumbled to myself in demoralized splendor.

Unfortunately, I was just a girl. A late thirtysomething cisgender girl at the hospital or the airport, a bull-daddy genderfucker in the kitchen, and a highly styled nymph with a huge strap-on dick in love and in bed.

"So estúpido . . ." I rambled beneath my lipstick application during one of my most suffocating follicular phases. My gender was simple: the inconveniently arcane hot girl straddling a stoic butch daddy with the best record collection during peak golden hour on a bed of carnations and a P-90 pickup to match her *harsh mellow.*

I downed a shot of Jager and grabbed the payment processing contracts to feel *responsible.* "I'm so tired of all the fucking boxes. I'd love a fucking contract that has a blank line for gender so I can put 'fucking tired-ass bitch from he—'"

"—space." Fulanito added a fuchsia rim along his usual jet-black eyeliner and spoke in a subtle, soft tone. "I'm going to be space cunt tonight."

"WERK!" We yelled and pounded our fists on the counters in unison, in delirium, to reconnect to the driving force we needed to perform at our best.

"HOLLA QUEE—"

Braden, a former militant for the alt-right and a renowned speaker for self-accountability, peeked back in. "Haha, pipe down fellas! Three more minutes!"

It wasn't that the fuchsia accent was so transgressive, so couture—it was just that we had finally laughed, truly.

We walked through the dimly lit corridor between the greenroom and the stage. It was just like 2112, when the Apollo, Terminal Five, Irving Plaza, and Kings Theatre had carried a sense of simultaneous glitz and home. I brushed my finger against the wall, and a striking déjá vu took me to the biggest stages and the biggest feats that had allowed me to be simultaneously known, respected, and well-paid, despite my internal wars.

During the Post-American Bloom, imposter syndrome became unnecessarily overrated. People had figured out that the keys to relishing in one's purpose were gratitude, mindfulness, and tranquility. They'd created great art, founded thriving initiatives for justice, had radicalized industries, and had rallied for feminist leadership that tempered the concept of competition. The Bloom had realized a system based on liberation, and people had found hope within it—as suspicious as it was to trust a republic with one's vulnerability. However, like we learned from the vast histories of counter revolutions and the subtle totalitarianism of their greatest gatekeepers—a self-congratulatory demeanor may heal your trauma, but it *will* kill the collective.

What's a traumatized girl to do when her band gets famous? I digressed.

Reaching the end of the hall, we disconnected from reality and became our songs. That was the trick to taking up space in complicated hellfire and conservative shitstorms for the sake of revolution—disassociation, mindfulness, divine disconnect. It's what paid artists have been doing for millions of years, whether it kills them or not.

Cheap Glitter took the stage.

There was a mist clogging the airshafts of our nostrils and eyes, fogging a reality where we were fighting for our lives as we were handed silver rainbow platters of camaraderie that should have been universal.

"WHAT'S UP, SPACE BITCHES!" Oracle yelled into her mic, and everyone cheered, clapped, and laughed as if we were clowns and crafty jesters attempting to steal the thorny crowns of the elite and failing. Nobody would turn a blind eye to farts and curse words, but we were invincible artists peeling the red tape from our eyes. We were the hottest queer puppets on the streaming platforms—a badge of honor for the Regime's facade.

Peering into the crowd amidst a mid-song crescendo where I typically pause and sneer or stare and tremble or moan—I caught eye of suits and oligarchs, teachers who betrayed us, and the toothy, well-tended smiles of a people who had lost all hope.

Tonight these songs were mere armor and grand gestures of protection. The pyrotechnics blared in a potentially seizure-inducing spectacle, and after one and a half hours of disassociated bliss, we closed the set.

"Wow. Well, that was . . . something?" I said as we headed towards the greenroom to recollect ourselves and pack up in relief, having made it out alive.

"I need to go for a walk . . . get into this long-distance reception . . ." Oracle walked out to the patio. "Come with?" She asked, and I followed.

We walked toward the scent of gardenias and lavender, through leafy sprigs of camphor, laurel, and hyssop, all under jurisdiction but free to smell. Oracle took my hand, and we danced on the greenery, getting lost in a whirlwind of success and justification. Oracle took her shoes off and stepped on the patch of grass adjacent to the bench-lined boardwalk that sparkled with that rampant quartz. I did the same, and we laughed.

"I haven't felt this in, maybe, two years?" Oracle pressed her toes between each blade of grass—raw, pure nature untouched by deforestation and nuclear assault, though still a little bit plastic.

Through the glistening distance, enforcement approached.

"Excuse me, this zone is off-limits to visitors." A security guard appeared between the tall, rosy stalks of crossbred florals.

"Sorry, I'll step off," Oracle was enthusiastic about settling into her breath every time she thought she might die. Oracle knew obedience was just another casually racist cultural chore in New America.

"You're going to have to come with us." Immediately, a string of law enforcement drones appeared from what seemed like nowhere, encircling Oracle and I as the guard handcuffed us with the kind of gentle, soft disposition that asks us to stand still or we might get shot.

Oracle was an exhausted warrior. I rolled my eyes, expecting a tired fear tactic. Law enforcement did not comply with my naive expectations; we were simply ushered into a sterile, damp hallway and placed inside opposite cells.

SHACKLES

America, old and new alike, loved to excuse punishment—whether through rejecting transformative justice, celebrating someone's imprisonment, or making a crush jealous on purpose. Having an utter lack of interest in understanding and healing all that is broken or convoluted was just the American way of life.

America did not want knowledge or peace—it wanted self-determination, self-care, and self-preservation. Punishment granted Americans the delusion of peace, as if peace could mean simplicity, boredom, complacency, and replacing long talks with thick air.

As prisoners normalized their guilt, pawns became self-loathing vampires, and victimized, lonely girls cut cords to avoid drama. Everyone is alone in the end.

In Sanctorum Custody, I could hardly breathe. I was handcuffed to a small iron bench with a cable long enough to reach the television remote and the meal receptacle. The television offered complimentary propaganda for life in the BioDome. Sanctorum Custody was a watered-down title for jail, kidnapping, and silent displacement.

The Creed of Sanctorum, often seen in propaganda, was almost like the pledge of allegiance when we were coming of age, thus memorized against our will.

"Sanctorum Custody is a humane response to minimal offenses perpetrated in the Great American Party's New American Regime. Sanctorum Custody grants the perpetrator a private space to breathe, think, and practice accountability in order to evade further harm. Sanctorum Custody is cruelty-free, and perpetrators are guaranteed freedom." I repeated it to myself in an effort to justify my rage and someday make art about it, given the will or access to live through this.

Sanctorum Custody, or SANC, was jail disguised as a barren Betty Ford Center, something that looked gorgeous but did not heal, soothe, or teach.

Flirting with a new level of numbness, I feared for Oracle's life. I waited for her like she was the only friend I had ever known and attempted to forget my own plight since that's what we Tati women did. We waited—for nascent fathers, for lost love, for internal healing despite a broken exterior. I waited as if it were my fault, as if it were my responsibility to set her free, as if I deserved this because I had signed the contract and I had accepted the payments on behalf of my legal name and I had written the song lyrics.

I wondered whether the rest of the crew were safe, captives, or navigating a new sense of fear. I missed the harshness of grieving everyone I had already lost. I missed fighting an impersonal war against the Regime from the stage—from the polyvinyl chloride, the printed inserts, and the static age. I missed longing for Fulanito. I missed the subtle stress that came with converting vegetable oil into biodiesel. I missed inertia and nothingness.

"Destroy, destroy, destroy! Remember . . . this is only happening because you're going to be some kind of example," I said, vacillating between speaking to myself and yelling into the ether. "Oh, the cost . . . of being a fucking sellout!"

SANC was a temperate sauna of concrete blocks with a wide skylight. The interior of the room was beige and wooden, like an overpriced day spa out of the twenty-first century. Earth tones and wind chimes were everywhere, intended to make SANC a calming yet infernal retreat. We were offered a twin-sized wooden plank to sleep on with a tufted headboard and Egyptian cotton sheets for comfort. The ceiling was lined with modern soft track lighting surrounding the art deco skylight and was adorned with Swarovski crystals for an extra dose of vitamin D. For this, SANC was classified neither as torture nor as a threat in society.

I thought Oracle could handle the neglect, the bizarre ambiance, the malnourishment—she was stronger than that—but maybe she couldn't handle the lack of control that came with this model of vague incarceration.

"Well if I can't eat, then I'll remember all those times I couldn't speak. I'll eat my shitty memories and my determination to get the fucking hell out of here." I forged strength, and I reminded myself that Oracle had a titanium backbone that had carried eight hundred years of ancestral resilience from the banks of Yorubaland to a dance hall in Trinidad and a kitchen table in Cleveland, Mississippi, where she'd laughed with cousins and learned from aunties. Oracle held her people in a towering regard, and I could not imagine this life without her.

MINOR OFFENSES

SANC provided a sense of disarray that could only be brought forth by hosting sterile accommodations that mimic spa-grade tranquility while simultaneously starving you and isolating you from your family. I spent the night waiting, spiraling, and numbing myself to sleep.

A day later, a nerve short, and with an outdated sense of rage and disgust, I woke up to a small white dish holding a soft, beige cream topped with cocoa powder and a mint leaf. I cried to myself and thought about every terrible thing that had ever happened and how I refused to repeat each one, and then I inhaled the mush—a bizarre texture, like that of a gelatinized vegetable. The food took me home to the tropics, to destruction, to an ending I was still processing, and to a beginning that was full of unkempt rage. The food was disgusting, but I forced myself to love it, as I had done many times throughout my life.

I closed my eyes, covered my nose, and swallowed. The tactic was easy. It only involved a little bit of cannabis in the system leftover from the day before a psychic vision of the magic that followed suffering, psychologically sucking in my taste buds, and *gratitude*.

When Florida sunk, we lost our cultures that had spread across continents, our agency, our lineage, and our romantic relationship to a socialist system founded by a social justice collective and destroyed by a fiber-optic devil. But mostly, we lost our families.

The Regime told the people to stop crying once they'd banned air travel and closed the borders to Florida. Our families had all been in their 90s, living in retirement communities, and enjoying their final years of creative outlets, lost love, and no worries. The Regime told us to note the disposability of *that* generation. Florida was mainly composed of a generation who deserved rest—sun, ocean, and freedom from the grind they'd dedicated most of their lives to. Rest, however, had no role in a new world where money, power, and advancement were precious while stillness and peace were obtrusive. Simplicity had no purpose in New America.

Fascism was a web of structural hypocrisies, and capitalism's hunger, communism's limitations, empire's worst intentions, and community's flawed elitism all fed the Regime where compassion went to die.

Now that green grass was the inaccessible fine wine to the knotted lungs of us bio-devastated Dystopians, we grieved a margin of ourselves that had been taken away too soon—the land, the soil, the interstellar connections between us and the earth. However, I bore the brunt of a front woman.

All front people are stricken with a plague to be a caretaker, to make sure everyone is on the same page, to make sure everyone is safe, though we'd often forget we were equally broken—just pegged as the loudest on stage. I saw Oracle as the loudest, the one keeping us in unison and from screaming in isolation. I was tired of screaming now. I wanted to breathe or smile.

I found comfort in knowing that this was the truth all along. Oracle did not fall apart like we did—not when her crush didn't call, not when her paycheck didn't come. We couldn't hear my scream without a mic, an XLR, a mixer, or earth-shattering acoustics, but we could always hear her backbeat—like a heartbeat. We couldn't make sound without it.

I felt held by my own convictions, like maybe I would be able to enjoy the frivolity of a crush someday. Maybe I would be able to evade my own trauma from loneliness, love, and body dysphoria and reveal this newfangled warrior, reinvented and redefined. This cliché resilient-woman hope that I'd pulled from the pages of a period piece about midwifery or suffragettes kept me warm in custody.

Minutes turned to hours, and the skylight became dark. I entertained these long nights as gifts. After all, my bones were tired from performing nightly, forcing poise and prowess, inches from Fulanito. I looked forward to losing my inhibitions and showing him my unhinged truth, and for now, I rest.

That suffering looked so gorgeous from here, so true and worthwhile was that suffering we chose for love or expression or survival. I prayed for Fulanito's intuition and for his safety. I prayed for Reggy to be sitting next to him, singing and laughing and learning that SANC was just another performative program for mild detention. Fear kept

me broken, but delusion was easy, as I had already convinced myself to believe in things like love and revolution.

I woke up to a horn blistering above me and interrupting a faux Regime sunrise peeking through the skylight.

"In accordance with the rules of the LGBTQ Coalition for Rights and Advancement, you have displayed both commitment to the Regime as well as profound showmanship. In gratitude and vindication, we welcome you to evacuate your cell. You will be escorted through the public halls for a go-round in the greenroom," the loudspeaker commanded.

I hurried out and caught a glimpse of Oracle in mid–jumping jack through the now exposed windowpanes on our respective cell doors. Crying and forcing a stealth demeanor, we followed law enforcement to the rest of Cheap Glitter.

We walked patiently in fear, in disgust, and in remorse, asking ourselves if this was the price of fighting beyond the parameters of familiarity. We were led to the greenroom.

"Hey, fellas!" Braden greeted us. "Let's circle up and have a quick go-round, alrighty?" he commanded. And to the dismay of our ancestors, we followed his instructions.

Oracle and I faced Reggy, Fulanito, and Ganache like pawns or lab rats forced to investigate how far we could stretch.

"Your friends are back to safety! However," Braden said, tapping his fingers perpendicularly against one another, "we ask that you be mindful when sharing any recaps on your performance at the Coalition and restrict any false narratives surrounding your time in detention." Braden was patronizing and dangerously vague as a pungent odor, like ammonia or aged cheese, permeated from his wool coat.

"Sure thing, Braden," Ganache interjected. "Can you let us know when to expect the van from the valet?" He silently farted beneath his baggy houndstooth slacks.

"Sure! I'm hoping within the next hour?" Braden obliged. "We would love to offer a late lunch buffet for you folks in the meantime!"

"No thanks, Braden—appreciate it!" Ganache replied.

"Gotcha!" Braden was flustered as we fished for either truth or chaos.

"Ah, one last thing!" Ganache was a white, tenth-generation Jewish Italian Muslim, a Taurus, and skilled in de-escalating unexpected racism without tears or reactionary displays of honest accusation. We often had to remind ourselves to let him speak when our words boiled beyond our lungs' capacity. "Are you able to provide any records or details on the arrest?" Ganache kindly asked.

"Unfortunately, we are not able to provide documents, as touching the grass is a minor offense that does not warrant documentation," Braden concluded.

"Are you fu—" Fulanito was an inch shy of combustion. "Are you aware that nobody said nothing to me? When I stepped on the grass?" Fulanito smiled at the officer.

"I, actually, am not sure of what you're referring to, Fool-aneato."

"So, like, literally, *this morning*, I was asking an officer about our friends as I was, literally, like, invited to step—"

"We actually didn't have any officers on duty this morning." Braden's tone drifted from a performative queer ally to a true officer.

"We'll have to wrap up soon here—did anyone have any further questions?"

"All good, Braden. If we can get any updates about our van within the hour, it would be greatly appreciated," Ganache responded.

We digressed and held one another close. Leaning back, I peered toward Braden from the corner of my eye as he swiped a glowing key card onto an ominous port beside the doorway. Enmeshed in a sense of doom, we packed up our things and exited toward the parking lot.

"We made you an altar!" Fulanito exclaimed while we hurriedly filled our bags with clothes, skincare products, and concessions. My eyes welled with tears as I pouted my lips, faced him, and grabbed his hand. Braden exited the hallway, and we let out a collective sigh.

"Holy fucking crap, Fuli, you almost got us arrested again!!" Oracle called him out with wide eyes and a devil's smile. We didn't know whether to laugh or scream.

We waited outside the venue steps at the valet pickup, and the Astra arrived in one piece. Service bots surrounded us, packing our belongings with unnecessary, inhuman precision. We piled in. That's the thing with Sanctorum Custody—we did not owe bail because we were celebrities, a cultural commodity. We were not offered information, just smiles and false notions of comfort. We could have become less profitable, less beloved, less famous. We could have disappeared. But this was New America—palpable, soft, liberal, fearmongers.

We exited the premises of the Coalition with no remorse or farewell and headed east.

"Wait, so did they give you any food?" Reggy asked.

"Sunlight and water." Oracle was depleted.

Sunlight and Water was the signature cleanse by the Regime's most revered Ashram guru, Stacy Kirkpatrick, who was from the Livonia, Michigan, New American Township—a suspicious backdrop for a suspicious peddler of co-opted South Asian medicine. Stacy's dietary practices enforced a cadence between bodily fasting and cultural cleansing—genocide disguised as *new wellness*.

"But the mush!" I interjected.

"I meditated that out of my memory." Oracle found peace.

We laughed and sighed and cried and felt that unique, jaded delirium that came with tour and civil unrest resulting in arrest.

In New America, "minor offenses" perpetrated by prisoners included walking on the grass, pouring non-H2O liquids into city sewers, speaking in an unpoised tone to law enforcement, speaking poor English, passing gas of any variety, placing recyclables and compostables in the trash receptacle, speaking with regional pronunciations—the list of expected obedience could go on. However, we knew the unspoken list, the list that included being poor, being Black, being disabled, or being a tired, uncouth woman on her menstrual cycle.

"There was just *something* about being offered luxury accommodations at the price of my own breath because I'm a Black woman on my fucking period enjoying the motherfucking grass." Oracle had come from nothing that had felt like everything. Her family's shared spaces, multiplicity of part-time jobs, and her hard-knocks reality had all reminded her that her family always came before material goods and industry.

Now, family felt auspicious, as if we were constantly holding on to our last breath on our last phone call to our last family member on the last island still habitable in the Caribbean.

"It was even an accident!" I puffed a joint and reminisced. "I'd just forgot it was against the law . . ."

"Queen! You were high as fuck!" Fulanito interjected.

"Bro . . ." We cackled with wet, obnoxious laughter. "Anyway, can we make sure the funds were transferred?" I wanted this to be over.

Oracle nodded, blowing a puff of smoke off her first blunt since being released. "Done! Now let's talk about something else."

Reggy connected his cellular device to the Astra lighter to access the internet, making sure our efforts had been acknowledged. Life in New America, away from East Dystopia and in the sheath of clean air, was a temperamental minefield.

"I even took my goddamn shoes off—it was so romantic." Oracle sighed towards the roving open road, and I leaned in, holding onto her left arm.

PART 2

JOURNEY TO THE END OF EAST DYSTOPIA

DELUSIONAL PEACE

For most of my childhood, I'd watched a new world flourish off the backs of our greatest revolutionaries. All the while, somewhere in a cave in middle America, the alt-right and their conservative elders had strategized in secrecy, rekindling fascism.

We knew this had been happening, but we were not prepared to lose. We'd chosen tour and music and free speech and rage because they'd come naturally, like curse words and bodily fluids. Our callouses were songs, however futile it may have felt to turn our emotions into weapons.

In the recent decades before it all went to shit, young and developing conservative generations had been formulating ideals that merged personal wellness, respectability, and site-specific environmentalism with class warfare, capitalist growth, antiquated structural racism, and good old misogyny.

By early 2116, the Great American Party was established through guerilla warfare and the destruction of a system too compassionate to survive. That year saw 365 days of fascists rioting under the guise of democratic socialism while squatting in the regions New America was set to destroy. By the fall of 2116, entire metropolitan epicenters had been bombed by the right wing, in order to colonize the center of the country with the BioDome, while the coasts had been gutted and flooded for natural resources. This was the war that had been painted by the historical and empirical self-determination that had destroyed Syria, Palestine, Ukraine, Afghanistan, and the Democratic Republic of the Congo. Mourning was every America's commonplace.

The *stronger* who'd survived the 365 days of rioting were just civilians, disguised as radical earth angels and the thousands of armed and tanked members of the right-wing army: the New American Defense.

After two hundred miles of winding concrete and particle intoxication that had kept Fulanito and I stupid and idealistic, we saw gorgeous, sprawling desolation. The tumbleweed summers and the decaying air quality were now respite—peace—a reminder of how gutted our bodies had been the morning after that unnatural disaster of New America. We'd held on through the idealistic eagerness to fight because we swore we knew how to rebuild. We'd learned from our ancestors that earthquakes were asking us to redefine infrastructure and industrialization. We'd known that hurricanes and wildfires were asking us to begin the elimination of deforestation and the fossil fuel economy in order to terminate the chaotic effects of global warming. We'd known our souls were at their best when we believed in love—and so, we gave our bodies what they'd asked for.

It was 8 p.m., and the sun had just set behind the yellow swaths of clouds. We'd been looking forward to idealizing the resistance and sitting on the dissent's new lump of cash as we escaped New America on our three-day journey back east through painful overlooks. Two hundred thousand dollars had entered the accounts of the movement, and as the energetic debris of the elite dissipated, I sulked in the ropes of my work. After all, achieving greatness meant putting everyone in danger.

Sometimes, I just wanted boredom, security that looked like waking up in the same bed night after night and breathing, living, suffering, hungering, determining, and dreaming—but always in the same bed. I wanted a semblance of home and no risks, just the stories of where I'd been.

The Regime was wholeheartedly but silently misogynistic and anti-Black. It had its rules, its sanctions, its lies, its red tape, and its loopholes, but the Regime's woman-hating and anti-Black rhetoric was foundational praxis. To the New American numskull, *women* were an umbrella for *gender variants*, just as *Blackness* was an umbrella for *non-white people*. Thus, women and Black individuals were pushed toward the ever-growing margins as American as apple pie and hydrogenated oils. Colorism and misogyny as a default influence was a hush-hush foundation unspoken of in treaties yet exercised in excess.

We were punk rockers, so *of course* we learned the loopholes, the dress codes, and the secrets that enabled us to perform to the gay fascist elite. However, we couldn't exactly know when racism would be embedded in the fabric of an oppressor—we just had to walk through life expecting it everywhere.

So, we expected racism, but $200,000 was now not enough.

We stopped at the first restaurant we could find and filled up our converter with the finest after-dinner vegetable oil south of un buen plato de Boliche. We were close enough to Dystopia, and we wanted history and revitalization.

That evening became a core memory and a catalyst in our return to what felt like desensitization but looked like peace. After we finished our meal, a sense of home crept from the swanky pines and the Appalachian sunset as we forgot what civil unrest sounded like.

"Awww . . . this is nice." Reggy was content and full as he poured the oil into the converter, like he was actually having some semblance of sweetness for the first time. Ganache was cheering him on like a gleeful little lamb in rusty Carhartts and Kool-Aid hair dye who may have just forgotten the threat of apocalypse.

We crashed at a nearby squat motel while we waited for the biofuel filtration to take place overnight.

The Hamhock Inn was a sanctuary between New America and East Dystopia, a midway point where we were greeted with warmth. We finally felt at peace sprawling in the parking lot, talking, fucking off, or doing absolutely nothing.

Oracle stepped barefoot on whatever remaining patches of green grass she could find and meditated, unbothered and confident, in a *hokey* and *delusional* metaphysical peace.

Like Reggie, I was also full. But teetering on the edge of despair was Fulanito, who was pouring over a new song in the back seat of the parked van. And then there was my heart that was teetering on the edge of emptiness and pouring over the memory of being held.

I stared at Fulanito from outside the vehicle to see what would happen, to see who would crash first and who would laugh last. Fulanito looked up with a coy smile and squinted in reverse—the kind of sultry, heart-palpitating glance that begins as the lower lash line is subtly raised and the upper eyelids rest.

I quickly turned away as a convoluted mess of butterflies and florals burst a little bit between my stomach and my pussy. I questioned whether I deserved what had just happened, the unsuspecting boner in my pants, the bellowing cry of an engorged clit who was trying to nap, quite frankly. Finally, I wanted to exit the pangs of PTSD, and I wanted to feel fiercely turned on without guilt or suspicion. I wanted to feel love without ice from past hurts, so I sat on a patch of grass with my orthopedic cushion, my thoughts, and my revolutionary fervor, like a sad gay Che on a chilly Sunday. I ignored Fulanito to my heart's content—while making sure I was flatteringly reflected in his rearview mirror.

At least tonight, we got to escape to normalcy. We rented a classic Muppet movie and ate food prepared by the Hamhock. Their cuisine sent us home, and we reveled in the black-eyed peas, alcapurrias, beef sautéed in tomatoes, achiote and *life* in corn tortillas, and jalapeño fucking cornbread sinking in its own sweat.

We slept for the first time in what felt like a month but had only been seven days of traversing wildfires and compromising our values to fund the dissent. Now we were back in Dystopia, piecing together the fragments of being artists, being revolutionaries, and being human. We slept in contentment, smiling, breathing, laughing in our dreams, and waking up to the blinding rays of the sun—our sacred star, capable of sustaining life yet too damaged to keep fighting.

The next morning, we sat by the lake and periodically put gas masks on our face while we circled a pot of coffee with the Hamhock patrons before heading back toward Appalachia, New Quakertown, the Northeast Corridor, and old New York.

Back in the van, we rode off, sulking in our respective post-war rebirths.

I WANT TO BREAK FREE

I knew about oil spills from my abuela, Ulta, who'd told me about her mother, my bisabuela, Amparo, who'd fronted bands during the twenty-first century and had played many an anti-fracking benefit with her rock band, La Otra. By the time Ulta was my age, she'd quit punk, found hope, met a guy, and gave birth to my mother, Tatiana; or as we referred to her, *Queen Tati*. My mother was raised in Ulta's commune, lending to her softness and avid sense of wonderment.

Oil spills were unheard of in my mother's generation. Until I was seventeen, the only chaos I knew was that of mending economic strife through the religion of mutual aid, and interpersonal social dramas. Maintaining Ulta's sense of hope was easy when there was so much proof that we, in fact, were on the right side of history.

LaVENDE
CLOV
GERANI
ROS
YLAN
BANYAN

Ulta's Asilio was a mystic swamp—a moderate rainforest, a palm tree that never stopped growing, an avocado tree that fed three generations, and an alligator sunning at the creek, unbothered by the metropolitan noise across the grass. But it was my Mamá's Asilio, Miami—free from the scathing homophobia Amparo had written about in her song lyrics—that was the place I'd go home to when old New York was too cold, when my chosen family was too busy, when my body was too sexless, when my heart was too iced from twenty years of not knowing love, when I was too tired or anxious, or bleeding on my chafing thighs and forcing a smile. This Asilio was a balm on the surge of getting older—the cracked tailbones and the trauma, the uninterest in superficial success, the unforgiving vulva.

My Mamá's Asilio was a humid, warm sheath of sunlight after having had thirty-five years of environmental regeneration. It was the cooling effect of the leaves of a banana tree holding space for my blood, my sweat, my suffocation from winter.

Asilio was home—gnats, hurricanes, tornados, sinkholes, alligators, and all.

But New York City was *life*. So, we stayed there during the riots, after the riots, and during the new regime. Our souls had been woven into New York's cultural landmarks during the worst revolution old America could have ever imagined, and yet we still foolishly believed the mystic swamp would persevere.

This trek was often for their memory—the flan, the coquito, the telenovelas, and the cascade of words that everyone called *interrupting* and Cubans called *speaking*. This trek was for forgiving Asilio—every broken memory, every nascent parent, and every unresolved fight.

I looked out the window and held onto my piece of larimar. The first time Cheap Glitter had made it to Florida, Fulanito had picked a piece of it out of the fine sand of the Gulf Coast and had handed it to me, effortlessly smiling and walking away. Larimar is said to carry the wearer's ancestors, spirit guides, and higher truth—these spellbinding notes of resilience that used to feel easy but now require a crutch.

Heading back east, we played a string of intimate shows, reinstating our sense of self, like maybe we weren't actual fucking tools. Maybe we could be forgiven sometimes, and maybe our intention to raise a shit ton of money for anti-Regime initiatives was valuable to some?

Next stop, the Appalachian fence.

Appalachia wasn't totally colonized—it was a minefield of potential New American policy and unsuspected law enforcement backdropped by raw, pure nature that'd been devastated by climate change and deforestation yet maintained by Indigenous stewardship. Within this vast area of land and dissent were small sanctuaries and sovereign cities. Tonight, we entered MayDay, population: *who fucking cares.*

Our venue was the James Hotel X, which had been built on the remains of the Old Virginias. Appalachia was dense with covens of permaculture witches marching along a range of rock monuments and endless seas of the last surviving pines Reggy had always talked about. It was breathtaking and ominous, quite different to the agricultural mini-mall it posed as on the World Wide Web for the sake of its own survival.

The internet as we'd known it was now criminalized and existed only as a basic telecommunicator with limited browser capabilities beneath miles of fiber-optic red tape. However, we'd been prepared for this American delusion, as New America was the playground of war.

The internet was home to simplified platforms for sharing tour dates, music, prose, art without the inclusion of *unwelcome themes,* and, of course, prudent event announcements for simple gatherings at the river or local cafes. But truth? Vulnerability? Despair? Not unless you wanted to revisit custody and maybe *die*.

This is why we needed hackers, masters of the dark web making sure our voice and our efforts spread. Hackers were abundant in this generation of despair. However, we were not hackers—not one bit. We were purveyors of traditional media and *very old* according to most hackers.

And thanks to the unrestrained barter economy that fueled the artist/hacker relationship, we'd been able to blast through a quasi-national tour.

Ganache was an old hacker, thank God, and we were grateful for him despite his harrowing tone and consistently jaded demeanor. He was tired of suffering—we all had something. Ganache had too much and did not want to vent about the body and mind that'd been stolen by patriarchal indoctrination before he could even speak. Ganache wanted to be our parent and fill the void of his parentless solitude that gave him claws at a young age as he grew up in the right wing districts. He was happy to take care of us, and we were happy to watch him hack.

The functionality of the internet depended on a sacred exchange between genius and deep-seated anger. With that, we pulled up into the mid-Atlantic smog like it was nothing, like the succession of empire was irrelevant.

We entered the James X and felt at peace once again.

"So, does your hair just stay like that in this dryness?" I asked Fulanito as we stood at the far end of the courtyard while everyone passed around chips and blunts. "Do you do a wet set?"

"No, touch it!" Fulanito said. I obliged, passing my fingers between his coarse magenta curls that shimmered against the cool blue fluorescents, creating a kaleidoscope of light. His hair was soft at the root and rough at the end—like seasons or fucking.

Dystopia suddenly paused to reflect on the revolution of my heart, but the cascading bodies blurred into warmth and energy. I did not care who was staring or who assumed my misbehavior, my unhinged nature. I was a witch, and I knew better, for this would all come crashing down someday.

But just for this moment, I was shattering time. I touched Fulanito's hair and crossed a line.

Exiting our echo chamber, we walked through the James's wooden pillars veined in moss and the unaffected faces inside—elated or disenchanted, we did not know—as a sudden surge of electric heat propelled us to the stage.

Locked into song and dance, our show at the James was convalescent. Wild-haired weirdos and mystical painted bodies reeking of sweat, beer, and mountain laurel yelled and danced and seemed to reconnect to the kind of levity that had been dead and gone in New America. Punk rock in its traditional, unpopular sense was present there in the broken speakers dangling by neon green ropes and wires and hanging above us like beacons—like death wishes. It was present in the lack of boundaries in the crowd, where wild, unbathed humans brushed against one another without inhibition or fear.

Oracle bashed the drumheads like they were enemies—or the state. She violently thrashed her full body like she had been reborn at the altar of a devil we all knew and loved. Reggy forgot his turmoil: his aching bones, inconsistent Dystopian healthcare, and intuitive rage. Reggy let an hour of yoga and a bellowing "GO!" ignite seven tangled melodic walks on the neck of his bass guitar, each unheard of to Cheap Glitter until now.

Fulanito got naked. It was the thick of his Saturn Return.

This may have been the best night of my life—I forget.

The light fixtures were opalescent but could have been skylights mirroring our souls to destinies we did not choose but were finally rehashing and understanding.

Appalachia was still a crystal mine, but no longer touched by industry. The structures that remained in these jagged, unkept lands had been reclaimed by the dissent. These lands were only accessible through dirt roads and clawed tire appendages needed to crack through burl and poisoned foliage. Spaces like the James X held and maintained regional cultures and their artifacts from bluegrass to blacksmithing. The James was part museum, part commune.

Tonight, however, was for creating a raging, awkward utopia. Fulanito stood naked and proud behind his saxophone, standing far too close to me while I pretended to be unfazed, because nudity was doldrum queer anarchy, and tonight, we were not going to make a fuss—although I wasn't able to speak to him.

I could not understand the wave of trauma that crashed into me whenever I was too in love, too turned on, too distant from the love I imagined, yet so close to Fulanito's tangible humanity.

I called it tangible humanity, but I meant his dick.

I wanted us all to be free. So, I ripped off my chiffon, and we danced in camaraderie, in commodity, and because the community loved a good, naked spectacle. Fulanito faced me and watched in fervor and heat, in batted lashes and mutual tension.

The community wanted power and reconnection to the body autonomy that toxic wellness had destroyed. So, we heralded a sensational blast of soul reconnection, of tits and ass and dicks and sass and unadulterated resilience.

FULANITOS CT TAKE UP SO MUCH SPACE
FUCKIN HIPPI
FINALLY FREE...
FUCK THIS!
Live Laugh Love Destroy!
GENDER IS STONE

Punk rock was a cultural phenomenon that had become quite distant from its initial groundwork, except in its commitment of truly loving and elevating and listening to thy neighbor. Punk rock was about picking one another up when we fell, whether it took seconds or years. It was this antigravity net that protected us when we were young and searching for a community with a history. On that night, it had been over 175 years since musicians had considered writing battle cries in the spirit of rage for communicating pain without a means to an end or for creating movements or communities. However, through 3-chords and very unkempt fury, punk rock was still the same old punk rock—an ancient portal into the underworld where the vague intersection between justice and freedom created sound.

But punk rock in today's revolution? In the slow-paced destruction of our homes and our definitions of security? Now, it was the universal token of Saturday night culture, not the underworld special it had once been. It was the floodgate of a subtle evolution toward a kinder world.

The curtains closed, and the crowd cheered. We'd done good, commodified or not. Still, my innards sank.

"Hey, come outside with me." Naked Fulanito grabbed my hand, and I did not hesitate—it was raining.

We danced and laughed, forgiving our sexual arousal, and forgetting the daily strain and the emotional grind. Fulanito danced with his eyes closed. Arms stretched across the ether, he was spinning, so I followed suit. He grabbed me from behind and spun me toward the sky, against electric fireflies and gently toxic rain. It was safe enough to dance and dangerous enough to fall in love. Fulanito faced me; our eyes fixed, and we spun in unison. I held on harder while the world disintegrated into a cyclical blur. Fulanito looked confused, his brows shifted from furrowed to asymmetrical to balanced and well-rested from traveling 20,000 miles, seeing his hometown in ashes, and watching me get arrested. In the dizzying spectacle, he smiled and laughed, and I did too.

I always wanted to meditate. I always wanted to quit the arts and focus on my community and my skills and create something beyond myself in the comfort of my own private, citrus- and patchouli-scented revolution adorned with pre-war ceilings and families of stray cats. Every now and then, I wondered who I was fighting for: the revolution and the magic we made by answering a calling, or Fulanito.

I never daydreamed of my success outside of knowing Fulanito. I mostly dreamed of my art and its purpose—what we would do next, outcomes aside. Fulanito wanted to be a fixture, and I wanted to place him there and keep him there so I could watch him smile from the sidelines or stand beside him on a faulty pedestal as long as it could hold his genius before it groveled at an elite class.

Fulanito was not yet my North Star—at least, I didn't think so. He was Saturn and Mars at their brightest because they required me to stay grounded, in tune, aiming for divinity, and out of my trauma.

We spun and spun and fell to the ground in hysteria. I looked at his face as the unfamiliar feeling of peace swelled.

"I don't want to stop." Fulanito whispered and possessed me. I grabbed his hands, and we were standing again—spinning—unaffected.

The crowds joined, and our hands clasped tighter.

We ran back in, looking for our pants, our gowns, and our wits as onlookers giggled into one another's embrace. Fully dressed, Fulanito seemed spent with feeling and walked toward another crowd that was funneling down from the show upstairs, away from me.

Maneuvering his way into the distant living room mosh pit at the lobby of the James, where punks caroused among the fog machines and tables of free fruits and anti-fascist classics, Fulanito found Silky, the forlorn genius who was supposed to have been my coconspirator but who instead became the one that never was.

Silky was not entirely guilty of her heterosexuality, but you can't hold a dyke's hand without expecting her to fall in love with you. I'd done just that when she'd drunkenly held my hand at dusk in West Dystopia on the hottest July in a hundred years. The year was maybe 2118—I chose to forget—and I'd been reeling for Fulanito while respecting the existence of Narnia, his partner, and pounding my exhausted skull against the concrete until I found a love that would give me attention and inspire me with great art.

Those were the days of filling voids and forging love in an attempt to accelerate a healing process that had made absolutely no sense to me.

Right girl, wrong time, I'd told myself when I'd decided that Silky could be the one.

Wrong. Silky was a heterosexual, or I, at least, was not butch enough. I'd worn a crewneck T-shirt that time at dusk when I should have been perusing great nature or secret spots but instead was searching for a girlfriend.

Flabbergasted for reasons beyond my control, I watched Fulanito flirt with Silky through the best of times and the worst of times, peculiarly creating a mirror to my fawning. To this day, I may never know whether his advances towards Silky were genuine or a mind game, as mystery is a beloved trope in the minefields of human affection. After all, Silky was not interested in me beyond casual girl-love and securing empty promises, so embracing Fulanito's affection was the undoubtable choice.

In the lobby, they danced and laughed and caught up in a way that should not have mattered. Friends gathered, the room was winding down, and Reggy trailed around. Dreadfully cognizant of the nebulous space between now and later, I ignored the scene. I wanted Fulanito to be free.

After a while of empty small talk with strangers in the other room, I followed Silky into the bathroom.

We laughed together for the first time in years, and I wished we could have been the young queer sluts who seldom batted a lash at chaos—youthful and free without the inhibitions of articulate wisdom—not because I was horny or missed her but because I missed that mask of resilience burgeoning queer sluts carried as a badge of honor. She smiled and sang my praises with submissive adoration, but I could not help but think that she may have also felt sorry for me in this solemn, polyamorous New York minute, when she'd rejected me to be Fulanito's dance-floor heroine. Tonight, I was only worthy of affection in theory. *Blah.*

Bodies and insecurities encircled the density of the room but did not play a role in reality as the music raged on. Nobody was there to fuck or run off or make plans; they were only there to sing along, hang out, and go home. I left the crowds, sat on the hood of the Astra, and sulked in the slim intersection between loser and important, getting gaslit by my intuition.

Over the James, the smog was clear and stars were visiting, but I could not find my sense of wonder. I smoked and sighed and raised questionable doubts based on fleeting moments and lies. Had he chosen to deny the moments of despairing affection that had felt like anchors, or was it just his natural inclination to forget?

The thing with twenty-second century wellness was that the ether was normalized.

In Dystopia, we'd maintained the energetic practices that we'd gathered during the American Bloom. We were telepathic, and we were psychic. We felt soulmates like we felt texture, like we felt breath. We were not superhuman, but we were products of a revolution that had turned worn, traumatized artists into fire-breathing prophets.

So, there was very little I could do about this lover's conundrum aside from choosing another path such as lesbian separatism or a new religion. But between our heartstrings and the doomed prophecies of home, the appeal of independence was bleak.

Fulanito and I were soulmates, I often believed.

We were also retired sluts without a net—horny, disorderly, and absolutely terrified of love.

The gang exited the James.

We piled into the Astra.

A WILD ORGY AND A FAMILY DINNER

Reentering East Dystopia and traversing Appalachia, the fresh smells of old trees and living soil held us. We were headed toward Dystopia's breadbasket, its farmland, smokestacks, food production, and fields of corn. This is what we had, and the unexpected patches of green were enough for now.

New America was not a religious right, but a harsh middle ground between forced wellness and autocratic fascism. By 2117, they'd gotten rid of trees and public art. They'd eliminated free healthcare, public parks, and basic rights. They'd ushered the Bio Zones into environmental warfare and had given us two options: *sink or burn.*

However, they couldn't get rid of that one thing that nagged at my arteries when I was learning to breathe, that gnawed on my eyes when I was trying to sleep, that thing that was smarter than me, that ate me alive and compromised my will to work or live. That thing that was so precious we desired it even despite a looming apocalypse. That everlasting syndrome that sits in my lower intestine like a bad meal or regret.

They could never abolish that unbearable signal from both the universe and our greatest self—they could not kill love.

Because love kept us believing and breathing and jerking off and hoping for *something* amid the awkward, polarized, daunting pile of shit that was 2121.

Still, I liked to believe the greatest love story ever told was the one about sleeping alone in a van, a squatter's luxury hotel, in old New York.

New York, with its half-destroyed skyscrapers, ancient bridges, mystifying limestone fossils, and cultural chaos seeping through the cracks of a devastated metropolis, is the home I feverishly missed on the wings of tour.

Heading back east in a sleet-covered van and armed with chaos appendages, a sigh of relief took hold of the atmosphere while Ganache swayed to vintage cumbia on the car stereo. Everything was back to *normal,* and sexual tension was once again potent and distracting.

The sun was setting, and the beauty of insurrection blurred into the past and the noise. It was like a purge, yet unintentional. Exiting one town and entering into the next, we'd leave behind the songs, the memories, the regrets, and the haphazard moments of staying human. In time, we'd forgive ourselves, one another, and the catastrophic, potential in-between.

Fulanito put on headphones and handed me the latter half of his Galletas Margarita two-pack. I opened my eyes, gasped, and smiled—doe-eyed and discreet—and he smiled in return in that five-to-ten-second tango that would live forever in my mind.

That night, we would play in Quakertown—a region that had once been known for conservative values and a subtle pace of living. Quakertown was now a reclamation of autonomous debauchery.

In Quakertown, everyone was hot and queer and covered in stick 'n' poke tattoos about their dog or their pain or their meds or something homoerotic.

Quakertown was simultaneously a wild orgy, a family dinner, and a silent meditation through sacred fields of corn.

Once we arrived, I sat in the van for what felt like seventeen days, though it was just an hour. I was having one of those post-traumatic flare-ups that raced between my junk and my heart until it released through my throat. So, I sat back and waited, catching a glimpse of Fulanito walking toward the venue. He caught my eye and smiled. I couldn't grasp these sublime flirtatious nods as reality, so instead, I mourned my sanity—and Florida, and girls with long hair and glasses, and queer brunch because I'll never be butch enough or polyamorous enough—and smiled back.

Bisexuality felt like an ancient curse, but I refused to rest or forget or deny my untethered truth. I did not care who the fuck you were or how long your hair or your dick was—as long as you were there, staring or singing back.

There was something about watching someone simply *exist* that could be deeply harrowing or deeply inspiring. I could see myself equally integrated or x-ed out, and I hated my ability to stay sound in whatever story my anxiety told me.

It's just that everyone in Quakertown was so fucking hot. I exited the van and walked toward an alley by the side entrance, where our gear was being towed on a shoddy ramp. I found a soft ledge with sprouting peonies and sat down, nauseated.

Watching Fulanito *exist* exhausted me if I let it. He looked so free, so self-aware, so sweaty and proud—maybe he was reeling from our performance at the James or from holding me or from something that should not matter if I ever hoped to find my own closure or peace. I was used to losing my spine, and this time was no different.

My spine often became exhausted around *hot* people. She wanted to fit in. She wanted to feel hot, too, in her chiffon, without being informed by ancient wounds, but there was always that sting of PTSD that, for some reason, would not leave me the hell alone.

If I could count the manipulative shots at my skull that I'd known too well, I would sleep better and be much better at counting. I'd had this one ex—I was about twenty—and he'd messed with my autonomy and my organs in a way that burned so deep. I'd committed myself to not over-processing that one era when I'd felt worthless, suicidal, inconvenient.

Because, oh boy, had I processed. I'd processed in therapy, in hot springs, in relationships, in funerals, and in the middle of wars, carnivals, and orgasms.

That night in Quakertown, my loose ends revisited. Whenever the trauma threatened to rise to the top of my brain, I'd drink more than my bandmates and I would on bad days. I often chose destruction when faced with any residue of those memories: the ones that made me feel wrong and undeserving of sensuality; the ones that sought clarity when the walls between Fulanito and I swelled; the ones that made me feel like a creature in the worst way—not the strong way like when I shit on the gender binary—the self-deprecating way like when I've lost all connection between my body when I touch it and my body in the mirror.

GETITOGE
CHEAP GLITTR

"CT, babe, can you even perform tonight?" Ganache passed by, tossing me my insulated water bottle. "How do ya feel?"

"I'm fine, goddammit." I hovered on a low ledge outside the Quakertown venue, slouching in my own phlegm that I had spit onto the pavement below me and watching my soul become enraged.

My soul did not want me to give so much attention to my trauma. My soul wanted my fierce alias to strut in front of the hot Quaker queers with neither remorse nor inhibition. My soul wanted to walk up to Fulanito without expectation, without wondering, *Who do you really want to kiss tonight?*

But doing so tonight proved futile. It was easy for me to sulk in public behind a deadpan facade that everyone assumed was just too stoned or just very, *very* inspired—on brand even.

Quakertown, on the other hand, was a burst of light. Sprawled between Appalachia and the mid-Atlantic coast of East Dystopia, the town was about 175,000 square miles of incandescent microcommunities scattered through farmlands and unincorporated highways.

Quakertown punk rock was a fast and furious underbelly with a carefree spirit that did not feel naïve, and tonight we would perform at its epicenter—The Shipwreck. It was about seventy miles outside of Philadelphia, a once metropolitan epicenter that had become a collection of small villages in abandoned, reclaimed urban landscapes with a vast focus on food and industrial machinery production. East Dystopia needed Philadelphia to eat, to breathe, and to have functioning medical centers and electricity—it was East Dystopia's holy smokestack. Outside of the city, however, were the remnants of western Pennsylvania, except without the segregation and the right-wing resurgence, there'd been no more flirting with New American values.

The scene here was not aggressive, questionable at times, but a respite every so often. The culture here was unsuspectingly *cleansed*, as if these people had spent the riots rehashing what was no longer necessary, meditating on it, making a knitted quilt about their inner findings, and then building for the dissent a sound culture of independent art and music without hierarchy or competition, without the jaded notes of coffee and piss that we romanticized in old New York while sitting in our morose demeanors and leather jackets. Quakertown was worldly and profound and culturally rich like a distant memory. It was Chinese, Ethiopian, Korean, Mexican, and Syrian: distant or unknown

CIRCLE PIT

In East Dystopia, West Dystopia, in anywhere except the BioDome, tourism was obsolete. We didn't visit our neighbors unless we had an essential task to perform—out of respect for our limited resources, out of fear, and out of global consciousness.

Tour, however, was god's work.

Performers of all stripes used touring as a means for transporting inaccessible goods or generating funds toward the dissent and for becoming vital sources of trade or therapy. To our shoddy exteriors and unkempt insides, this life *was* the dream—despite the sleepless nights, the long drives, the despairing accommodations, and the faulty electrical circuits that were no longer the fossil-fuel-free, fiber-optic renaissance they'd once been.

Exhausted from watching his Appalachia deteriorate from catastrophic rises in heat and humidity, Reggy pined for his most recent caress. Equally lovelorn, Reggy was the one I related to the most when I sulked in my emotions.

Oracle was a teacher—my oracle. Fulanito was a guide—my muse. Reggy was my late-night cheesecake.

"Dude, I am freaking out. Can we go cry?" I asked Reggy as I caught him on his way into the venue.

"Ha! Come on, CT, you're about to scream about it." We laughed, and I digressed.

"I noticed Fulanito hanging with Silky yesterday," I told Reggy in mild shame. "I wanted to die but did yoga instead."

"That sucks . . . mostly because it's pretty normal." Reggy was profound with observation. "Like caring is pointless, but the principal is draining."

"I know." I took a drag off the tiny, purple glass chillum I kept inside an interior pocket of my denim vest. "Nothing would matter if we could just be this totally well-rounded polyamorous couple with zero trauma." We laughed at miracles.

"You ask for soul mates—you get bandmates."

"Bro . . ." I put my arm around Reggy, and we scrambled back to the venue. "I love you, man."

Entering The Shipwreck, we were faced with a throng of punks and clowns and wild displays of self-expression. Reggy pulled me to a corner to recollect ourselves before getting lost in the chaos.

"Hey, so, guess who's gonna be here tonight . . ." Reggy had a pen pal in Quakertown, one he'd used to fuck under the fireflies and the crescent moons of Appalachia, before the Regime.

"No way! So cool." I knew he was referring to Gemmx. The two were not committed but had exchanged years of affection. Gemmx was probably sewing a horse head mask out of trash or cooking dried legumes with a mysterious plant they'd found somewhere because they swore it would prevent scabies but also make your piss blue.

"Hell yeah." Reggy returned a deep, knowing smile, and I shook him in enthusiastic accord.

"Hey so, did you see Fuli gave me the second Margarita?" I asked, half shamefaced, half unabashed.

"What is wrong with you people!?" Reggy laughed, and I smiled in return with a cynical, fart-faced grimace. He grabbed a couple of glowsticks from the complimentary stash and searched for Gemmx through the punks, the drunks, and the ravers coalescing before the stage.

Sure, notions of peace and tranquility from ancient Quaker thought permeated through the mid-Atlantic, but Quakerpunx were eager to scream and fuck and spit glitter into our eyes—pink glitter because here, we were sapphic and delicately in tune to nature. The Lehigh Valley adapted the Quakertown name after the Quakertown /Exit 44" sign off of Interstate 476 was struck by lightning and toppled into the Regime's regional courthouse, destroying the structure that had decided the mid-Atlantic's dystopian fate.

As stealth, concrete New Yorkers, we marveled anyway at the release that this peace could bring.

I sat with Oracle and Fulanito on a displaced back seat of a Chevy Suburban that sat on the corner of the basement venue. Everyone gathered near, bringing us weed from their garden and bagels from the trash, accented with an array of vegan cream cheese flavors in assorted seashells and petri dishes. The Quakerpunx were caretakers and confident matrons.

"Ugh . . . I love the lumbar support on these seats!" Quakerpunx were also my trigger. "I think I'm just going to sit until we play."

"What the fuck's up, Queens! Welcome to The Shipwreck!" Pants Crusher entered the scene, and we squealed like lost kids. Pants was the king of mid-Atlantic DIY but, as an anarchist, felt very uncomfortable when faced with the reality of his power and investment in maintaining a music community. Pants was just shy of twenty-one but had already built a movement, from the basement of The Shipwreck.

"How's tour?" Pants asked, winningly and enthused.

"Oh god . . ." I was not my best self.

"Let's just say we're so happy to be here." Oracle raised a glass, and we toasted against every recollection that made the system feel larger than the galaxy. "To here!"

"The James show was sick, though." I mumbled.

"Yeah, that was fierce." Oracle smiled.

"Yeah, Fulanito got na—"

"Hell yeah. Thanks for making it out here. We—" Pants saw something in the distance. "Oh crap, y'all have to meet Sandy; she's over there! She had a dream, with sleep paralysis, about the show. You know how she is."

Oh, great, I thought to myself in a self-deprecating tone fabricated by my worst abusers who did not want me to feel powerful, a tone set by the ghosts of my ancestors who never wanted their wives and daughters to thrive, a tone that suggested competition as a self-fulfilling prophecy in order to prove that I'm *pretty fucking cool* or that I'm *at least* worthy of existing.

Sandy was a legend—and I was kind of jealous.

We all knew she existed and that she cast spells and made deals with all kinds of devils while holding space for all kinds of angels. We knew she was part of Demonixa, a punk rock coven made up of Brazilian,

Sicilian, and Caribbean healers. They did not share secrets or potions unless the universe demonstrated and begged for the work that only they were capable of crafting.

Before New America, Demonixa had all been baristas, clowns, sex workers, and scientists because they could not sell magic due to a karmic agreement with their past lives as Samhain's Encanto. Encanto had been a turn-of-the-century coven who had not honored their pagan guides and who had appropriated and sold their Indigenous constituents' secrets. Thus, these secrets had been passed down to Demonixa through the ether, through their strongest ancestors, but with a toolkit on and a charge for karmic justice.

Sandy was born exhausted and jaded and had spent her life gathering taboo skills that were a test against Encanto's fallacy. Sandy was also saccharinely joyful to the detriment of every morose white boy punk rocker. She was Demonixa's Sicilian contingent, the past-life descendant of Katherine Marie Claire—who'd been the leader of Samhain's Encanto—and the culprit of the curse that had founded Demonixa's purpose.

Demonixa had allowed themselves this lifetime to herald a path of compassion and to heal and transform the earth through their supernatural abilities—telepathy, precognition, clairvoyance, telekinesis, astral projection, and *allegedly* teleportation.

Demonixa's role in New America's dissent was to do better. They were the essence of everyone and everything I wanted to be: calm, in tune, fun, aware of ancestral purpose, magical, gorgeous to the naked eye but a kaleidoscope of history and wisdom to the intimate partner, very inspirational, typically in a flowing gown, often found by the sea talking to dead people and writing songs, horny, very horny, also jaded, and therefore very in love—not to a detriment but at the pinnacle of an enlivened heart space.

Yes, that was the me in my fantasies, in my vision of post-traumatic resilience, on good days in West Dystopia, and on a balcony overlooking the glow of toxic phosphorescence. That was the me before they'd starved us, before I'd witnessed the death of Appalachia and gotten too close to New America, before they'd fried me from within—the me before the unpleasant withdrawal that came with the initial descent of a national tour.

This perception of self was rare, and I saw it in Demonixa, in most of the Quakerpunx as well. Their powerful and wise eyes and their uncanny ability to hold onto peace during collapse was evident. I wanted to be that—to offer that.

"Hey! I'm Sandy!" She walked toward me, as if we had always known one another, and I stood up to greet her.

"Wow, hey! I'm Carolina, or CT if you're tired."

"It's so cool to finally meet you!" Sandy had been following and supporting Cheap Glitter for over a decade. "Can I show you something crazy?"

"What's that?"

"I can tie my labia in a knot! Wanna see?"

"Hell yeah!" I exclaimed. This was just art, and onlookers surrounded me. Sandy lifted her pleated pink polka-dot pleather skirt and pulled out her labia while laughing. Like an offering, she presented either lip in unison. "See?"

This was not sexual; this was not awkward; this was *Quakertown*.

Sandy resumed stretching out her labia as far as possible and then tied them in an overhand knot, as promised.

"Ta-da!" Sandy presented her work with pride. Oracle and Fulanito watched from beside me, and locals whispered, "She's doing the thing for Cheap Glitter!"

"Wow! Bravo!" We cheered and clapped, and Sandy bowed for the momentous response, likely taking a second look to ensure our circumference was adults only.

"Thank you, thank you." Sandy was a rare Gemini stellium: a Gemini Sun, a Gemini Rising, and a Gemini Moon. We did not know what to expect—sincere wisdom and practicality, or a very horny clown.

Sandy helped me lose inhibitions. I reached a sobering pace as we talked, and we danced in the crowd to the other bands. Fulanito side-eyed me and my independence for a minute that felt eternal, so I reminded myself of all the times he didn't have it in him to talk, to go for a walk, or to hash out the inconsistencies of the last four years and move on or fall in love. I forgave whatever *was* in him and danced.

For the night, the unsavory accents of my obsession with Fulanito waned—my trauma dissipated. It felt adult—*healthy*. Fulanito danced with those freaks over there, I danced with these freaks over here, and we both remained suspiciously confident, although not confident enough to take risks or make mistakes—not enough for a breakthrough but enough to dance in my bones and with some cool dykes in some rusty brick-and-mortar mid-Atlantic warehouse that smelled like yeast and lavender.

I left the crowd carrying my satchel of gear to find myself.

"New York, ay?" Sandy sat next to me outside the warehouse while I was tuning my guitar on the brown brick ledge that surrounded a bed of hemlock.

"Hell yeah." I looked down toward my guitar. "New Yawk."

I was so fucking *cool* when I wasn't in love, when I wasn't weak and hyperaware of the cosmic significance of a blank stare. This experiece made me sensitive to witches and clairvoyants, and that made me bad at discerning ego.

“I grew up in Atlantic City! I’m pretty much a mermaid,” Sandy confessed.

“Is that right?” I was reserved and terrified. Sandy had V-shaped fuchsia bangs and a buzz cut in the back. She was tall and beautiful and interested in talking to me. “So, when’s the last time you went in the ocean?” I asked with sparkling curiosity.“

Oh fuck . . . probably before the riots. Is it really green?” Sandy remarked with suspected disappointment, having been born and raised in the ocean.

“Yes. It’s kind of nice to look at . . . when you forget what it feels like to swim.” I mirrored her dissatisfaction.

Sandy stared close and unfurled a sympathetic prophecy. “Hey, you should come out to the Demonixa van after the show!” I gasped and smiled and did not say a word. “Don’t tell anyone, but I think we have something that you need.”

I wasn’t sure whether this was about drugs, sex, or rock ’n’ roll, but I obliged.

Cheap Glitter took the Shipwreck stage—in awe, in stupors, in bright tulle borrowed from the free boxes lining the corridor where our merch table sat. Local distributors of clothing, food, handmade essentials, and art joined the carnival because Quakerpunx were geniuses at merging worlds.

Raging in Quakertown was like downing glitter bombs and soda from the fountain of youth. It was wild hairdos, wild capes, adults dressed as clowns, punk rockers and their children bursting with wildlife, and bagels. There was something about bagels and their abundance, their simple production, and their overcrowded factories. The Quakerpunx loved tossing bagels around—some would get eaten, and some would get tossed out of reach to the dismay of performers.

The children were usually kept at bay from drunks and labia art and the consensual garden fucks of our horny, rabid dissent. On stage, however, we put our vices, our stigmas, and our secrets aside, and we all danced together as a family, living—since we had forgotten how to.

Through the bodies and chants, a costumed centaur bum-rushed Reggy, knocking him over and spilling gin all over the neon pink and purple speaker cabs, only to reveal the one and only, the elusive Gemmx.

Gemmx was an anomaly, a strange bookend to Reggy's saga, a luthier, a carpenter, and tonight, a centaur.

The speaker cabinet feedback squealed into disparity. Noise and laughter chewed us up and swallowed us and took us into the threshold of our own doing—a sanctuary as a basement in the middle of somewhere electric.

"Alright. Fucking Quakerqueefs . . . shiiiit." Fulanito lead the Quakerpunx into a cadence of sweat and squeals. Every song was a miracle and a riot.

"Circle pit!" Fulanito commanded.

Circle pits were ceremonial, an undying twentieth century tradition. They happen in mosh pits when the song reaches a pinnacle or a breakdown, and tens to hundreds of people coalesce and make a giant, infamous, empty circle. As the members of a circle pit wrangle profusely, at lightning speed, the performer receives a bolt of inspiration. Sometimes people would fall down or break an ankle or get trampled

FUCK THIS
LONELY

by unaware battering rams of people; it didn't matter, though, since there were always spectators maintaining the peace.

We played our last song along the cylindrical engine the circle pit fed us. Cheap Glitter closed the set a little after midnight, and we packed up our instruments behind the sequined curtain to the left of the stage. Ganache and the Shipwreck crew were on top of it, so I trailed ahead.

I followed Sandy Beerbrat to her van for secrets, drugs, or an exorcism—I was unsure.

DEMONIXA

I had never been close with this kind of witch before, the kind with deep roots in her ancestral purpose yet who was also active in the subcultural underground. Sandy's father was Sicilian, by way of Atlantic City, but her family was chosen up and down the coast by her eagerness to heal the unwarranted chaos of karmic debt. She had no recollection of her birth city but carried eons of past-life storytelling in some deeply concealed vessel between her brain and throat.

"Over here!" Sandy led me to the Demonixa van where the potions and retributions were packed and stored for lost and willing souls to partake.

"What is all this!" I entered the sacrament.

"It's kind of like . . . everything."

"Hey, hey, queens!" A few voices floated out from behind a silk, rose-colored curtain embroidered with gold lamé and diamonds.

I stared at the glass statues, the fresh florals, the dead florals, and the colored candles in odd shapes, both lit and spilled on pages torn from sacred texts. The smells of burning cedar and burning dinner danced from the shelves to the exhaust that was pumping biodiesel into the still Quaker breeze. I saw my future sprawl before my inhibitions, my insecurities, and my one-track mind running backwards to last month on the balcony of the Jack.

"¡Oye, mija!" It was Forever—For-fucking-Ever—the punk bruja who had slayed the dragons of patriarchy and pretty much transformed the global networking collective that had spawned after the death of *functional* social media. Forever had turned our enclave in the dark web into something universal as opposed to a bunch of isolated techies sitting around talking shit about the Regime.

"Carolina!" Amaranthine peered from the curtain.

Shaking in my boots with a delayed reaction, I couldn't believe I was with this coven—in this moment—being treated like a champion of some other walk. Here, I wasn't a failure at love or awkward and uncouth—I was divine, an untouchable artist. In here, I was alone for a reason. I was learning the ropes of a trajectory that could only hold the lonely, the angry, the resilient, the self-deprecating and the self-sabotaging: front women.

We embraced and laughed and reminisced about the last show Cheap Glitter had done in Quakertown not long ago, when Quakertown was easily accessible by the raw, clawless tires on our beloved Astra III.

Amaranthine Simões was the curator of pretty much everything that had ever led me to believe that this fight was valuable and necessary. She was the organizer of Black Moon Con, a two-week conference addressing the Regime's destruction. Amaranthine radiated leadership, education, transcendent eagerness, clairvoyance, and the ability to hold sources of power accountable. Black Moon Con was renowned, respected, officiated, and attended by leaders of higher education that had found a clean respite in the Regime, albeit a respite that had compromised their free will. Black Moon Con had converted enough leaders of the Regime to prove that another world was actually possible.

Forever and Amaranthine inspired and scared me because I did not feel like a witch. I just felt like a punk rocker—a party girl, a weirdo, a kind of psychic daughter of revolutionaries who was very good at matchmaking her friends—and a bruja who carried light conversation with her ancestors.

My ancestors and I bickered, and we sang songs, learned recipes, and laughed at men. They cleared crossroads and forgave my mess since I was undoubtedly on a mission. But we did not complement one another in the divine ways that these witches complemented theirs. These witches could read tarot cards and had relics and potions and history and connection that was not marred by the Regime. I was just traumatized—a bitter bitch in a rock 'n' roll band who just wanted love.

"Hey y'all, sit around! Come chill by the fire." Forever walked out with three cups of coquito made from the finest coconuts of a still breathing South Pacific coast of Kali where Forever had made the daunting trek, more often than not, to perform miraculous healing work. "So, mija, how's tour?"

We sat in a circle on the carpeted van floor, on different-sized cushions covered in checkerboard and floral-embroidered velvet throws. The window overlooked the rest of the world, the pine trees, the warehouse, the string lights, and the effortless beauty of people having a good time.

"God. Ridiculous. I mean, don't get me wrong, the shows have been amazing. The west is really beautiful. Appalachia was fucking wild.

VIDA
Salt

We've raised over 450K in New American dollars for the movement to stop the privatization of East Dystopia!"

"Hell yeah! Congrats!" Forever responded, genuinely attuned. I shrugged.

She added, "So, what's so ridiculous?"

"Ugh. Me and Oracle got fucking detained—in Trust," I told her begrudgingly, yet jaded and complacent. Arrests in the Regime included a non-disclosure agreement and penalties for exposing the details of Sanctorum Custody. Forever gasped and threw her body backward with a sudden shock that I hadn't seen yet, as the band had kept it to ourselves until now.

We did not have the capacity for judgements and concern; after all, *we* had chosen to compromise our morals and our safety for the sake of uplifting the movement.

"We did it for $200K, but I don't know if that was worth it. I can't believe I put her through that for money."

"Damn, C, I'm so sorry to hear that. You were both great tonight!" Forever said.

"Thanks. She's invincible."

"Hey!" Amaranthine pulled her tarot cards from her dress pocket. "I'm going to pull some cards for you." She shuffled with her baby blue stiletto nails, short enough to pull and long enough to cut you. She was generous and divine and did not mind schooling my alleged thick head.

Amaranthine continued to shuffle and smile while Forever and Sandy sat on either side, clutching their fists and knowing that, perhaps, a lobotomy awaited. I wasn't scared—I was used to dead-end prophecies and harsh realities. I really just wanted to know about Fulanito, anyway.

“Okay. So, we know it was hard that you and your girl got detained. But listen . . .” Amaranthine spoke in both jest and hard-to-swallow pills. “It’s not about your tour, your plans, or your agreement to play Trust. So, chill the fuck out.” Amaranthine pulled the Five of Swords and the Three of Swords, shedding light on the grave I constantly dug for myself.

“Stop wallowing in this guilt. You need to step the fuck up without romanticizing that *sad cunt energy.* Don’t be a light-skinned Latina martyr type. Step out of that unnecessary guilt, that Three of Swords cave of trauma.” I nodded and felt the cool rush of a slap on the wrist soothe me like a craniosacral massage. “Your grieving is done. How do you expect to be strong for your band when you’re acting so beholden to others’ trauma?”

I nodded again, wondering whether there could be a cure-all for both PTSD and our own bullshit.

“Next, you have to stop worrying about him.” Amaranthine pulled the Lovers and the Six of Wands. “Again, you have to chill the fuck out. Show up at your parade unbothered.”

I cried and wondered whether I had finally arrived. “The thing is though . . .” Amaranthine pulled the Tower card. “You have to burn down this foundation. It’s a cycle of karmic violence. You may have lied and burned in your past lives, but all these scabs are exhausted—they’ve had their time. You broke a curse. But you can’t keep spiraling and rehashing and internalizing every shitty thing that happens—we’re in a revolution. We don’t even have the time!”

Forever rubbed between my shoulder blades where trauma sat like a barnacle. I rubbed beneath my eyeballs to de-escalate the swell of tears.

“But in order to get there, you have to release the rage.” Amaranthine pulled The Star. “You have to pursue reinvention and heal from something that happened fifteen years ago with the person who taught you how to believe in sexual prowess and then who took it back through violence and coercion. And now . . ." My eyes swelled with tears, and Amaranthine was affirming.

"Now you are just angry." She pulled the Nine of Swords. "You know what needs to happen, but it involves extracting the greatest wounds that keep you full of rage. The wounds that keep you as this character you created, this sexy, shiny wound that the crowds adore, that the people need, and that you are fucking sick of." Amaranthine looked into my eyes with piercing conviction and paused. "You are ready to be free, to love your life, to step into the revolution with some kind of armor that isn't about the gashes but the light, the ether, the power you can have beyond the simple human connections of art and money." She pulled away and took a sip of her coquito.

"Mm-hmm." She smiled toward me. "Are you alright, babe?"

"Yes. Oh, yes. Please. Thank you! Give me more."

"Well, it's time for you to see the artist other people see."

"Goddammit."

The trio laughed. Dusty images of practical wellness routines raced from one side of my brain to another, and I was now looking forward to finding someone—anyone—who was remotely excited to talk about this kind of stuff.

"Except you deserve to fucking heal from some dickbag's bullshit!" Amaranthine continued.

"Fuck!"

"Fuck yeah!" Everyone pushed me around, rare joy radiating as I shook from side to side.

"So you can grieve the real bullshit with a clear mind." Forever de-escalated us. "You're grieving Florida—family."

AGUANTE ME

In theory, I was ready for this—as a super cool, creative freak who tried to use her powers for the sovereignty of humanity—but in practice, I wanted to take another drag of the weirdest, longest joint with a dab of god-knows-what, or maybe I wanted another seven minutes in heaven on a balcony with Fulanito.

I guess I am a healer? I thought to myself, simultaneously questioning how I could fake it in the meantime.

I had always walked through life as if I were so beyond this—so aware of my purpose—despite the claws of my cunt and the knives of my heart cutting me fifteen years ago, creating a lasting fog over every palm tree I wanted to miss.

Every time Fulanito was away, I swore I felt his breath—always close to me even when afar. When I yearned for him, it provided the illusion of healing. I needed to breathe on my own, run wild, and act free without the rage that'd sat inside of me since the last time someone had said *I love you*. It had been about fifteen years since. I'd been in shards and discontent in the back of a Greyhound bus that smelled like urine, but I hadn't cared because my love's hand had been inside of me, in a waking body surrounded by golden hour and blinded by a silent, stylish, heartrending monster.

His name was Pluto, and he'd been, like, the *king* of the anarchists.

Or just a brain-numbing, mystic heartthrob. I chose to forget—I just remember that I'd loved him. He'd made me the self-deprecating *artist* I'd thought everyone saw me as—revolutionary, yet cynical enough to make 'em laugh—a *very* sad clown.

"I'm sick of it." I recoiled. "Give me the hard shit."

"Oh, that's not my job, Cubanita." Amaranthine practiced Candomblé, a denomination of Vodún, which meant that she did not commune with neither my ancestors nor visiting spirits. Regardless, my spirits—at home in the islands just north of her home in São Paolo—were survivors of the same genocide but purveyors of a different pantheon.

On the islands of Cuba, Puerto Rico, and the Dominican Republic sat mine and Forever's ancestors: laughing, undeterred, sipping cafecitos and coquitos, and scoffing at their broken dreams because every fracture revealed a new, sacred path.

"Come here—I'm going to make you un cocimiento." Forever pulled me toward a tiny stove.

"Oh, I'm not thirsty."

"No, it's going to be three separate baths that you will bathe in when you get back home—resurrect that shit."

"Oh, my god!" Sandy peeked from behind the rose curtains. I smiled at her in a daze. "This is what I told you about!"

"One is for fortifying your acceptance of what has to go, one is for releasing the trauma, and the last is for embracing the healed version of yourself." Forever was initiated in the Ifá practice; she came from generations of priestesses who had transformed complacent subcultures into havens for marginalized people looking for a home. We had originally met over eighteen years ago at Black Moon Con. She'd come up to my cesspool of messy kids in butt flaps and cheap lipstick that were giving each other shitty bangs with crinkle-cut craft scissors, smoking lavender spliffs, and eating dumpstered peeps. Forever would never have done such a thing—she had figured out hair, scissors, self-love, and the dangers of refined corn syrup in an *adult* way that did not seem punk rock at first glance but was divine and telling. She had been following my band for years, but I was always a little bit intimidated, always on the sidelines when she was around.

I sat in the back of the van while Forever boiled premade blends of flowers and bones and palos in opaque liquids invented by her abuelas. Three separate pots sat on three separate burners. We watched and danced to digital cumbia on the radio, unaffected by the fact that according to this magic, I may never be this frigid again—this conditioned by my rage.

"So, this is it!" I couldn't be more grateful that Forever saw me the way my fans saw me, but I guess, this was it?

"Let's let these cool down for a few minutes," Forever said. The liquid in the pots had reduced to a small, concentrated puddle.

I was unable to sit in that power, to wear that crown of thorns and roses and spikes and unicorn horns and walk around as if I were the coolest shit since hot chips. Forever poured the three boiling mixtures into three separate two-ounce amber-colored jars and aligned them around a small yellow fan that was clasped to a windowpane with fake pink florals and purple tulle.

"Why still so amargada, babe?"

"I'm just kind of in love, I guess?"

"Oh—I heard."

"Yeah. It sucks." Amaranthine's reading had clearly articulated this shameful, embarrassing reality. "It's just not the shits and giggles I've heard about in rom-coms, you know?" I was sitting in one of the tender moments we all dream of: I was in a slow-paced, awkward, mutual crush with a coconspirator—a coworker, a bandmate, a flatmate, a voice I had loved since I'd first heard it a decade ago—an emotionally unavailable star-crossed sorcerer who sat beside me every night but looked away and only glanced back on occasion. It was a learning experience, I guess, a lesson in reclaiming the broken parts of my past that still festered in my present.

"Well, that's what the baths are for! To clear the fog, to heal from Pluto, from the Regime. You just have to trust."

"Ay . . ." I cried again into Forever's embrace. "Thank you, Tía."

Forever bagged the cocimientos, now a gelatinous, leafy paste, and placed them in a small velvet box for me to take. From the side window, the show's crowds had dispersed, and I noticed my band shuffling around, yelling my name.

"Caroliiiiiiiiina!" Oracle and Reggy perused the fields.

"There go your peeps . . ." Amaranthine squinted and smiled toward the window.

"CAROLINA! TATIANA!" Fulanito had a way of effortlessly dramatizing everything. "¡Mi amor!" He belted a despairing cry in the distance. "¡No me hagas esto!"

"Did that fool just . . ." Amaranthine suspected flirting.

"¡Aguanta me!" I panted with a wide mouth and furrowed brows, shaking my hands, and bouncing up and down in an awkward disarray that let loose the lost cannon in me. As I was wailing, Demonixa rallied beside me, jumping up and down and shaking me. I had risen, above the trauma and the disbelief.

Albeit, annoyed. "¡Pero ques eso!" I cried out.

"Get it girl." Forever toasted her glass of coquito to the heavens.

"Pero why . . ." I continued to jump with both hands holding onto my skull.

"Yeah, shake those titties!" Sandy yelled, and I fell to my laughter in revelation. I felt the sacred crevice widen and the untapped trauma divulge. My despair started to feel like performative disbelief—not because this love was not real, but because I was finally accepting that maybe it was.

"I think I hear them." Oracle heard us from the field, and the crew walked toward the Demonixa van and our yelling.

"Oh, hell yeah. She's probably getting a limpia!" Oracle had been suggesting these kinds of cleansing methods for a long time. Her love language was exploring the metaphysical properties of rocks and minerals with esoteric femmes and attempting to live beyond the realms of nuclear families and traditional love. She'd wanted this for me.

That sounded divine and all, but my love language was breaking shit and masturbating in storage closets. So, I guess I was ready for something more.

"Don't forget to find us when you come back!" From inside Demonixa's van, Sandy waved from the altar in the back, and Amaranthine raised my hands and did a dance. I joined to the tune of nothing—a clear path.

"Call me after you do the limpia!" Forever waved, and I walked toward the front door.

"Thank you, everyone, goddammit. Thank you. I don't even—" Demonixa rushed toward me. We embraced and cried together, looking beyond Dystopia and forward to a world where we could traverse mountains and swim in oceans.

I walked out of the van to find Cheap Glitter waiting for me, like they were proud, like they knew more than I did. Ganache was carrying a bin of merchandise to leave with Demonixa, because while they don't sell their magic, they could accept our offerings.

"This isn't much, but thank you, again." I dropped off the box and headed out.

"Oh, hell yeah. I get the leather thong!" Forever rejoiced in the distance.

TOO MUCH PRESSURE

How easy it was to believe that I deserved those great walls between me and my resilience—because I fell in love with Pluto and made a complicated choice once?

New America's doctrine on mental health deemed reactionary responses to oppression as more oppressive than the oppression itself—as stated by President Abaddon. Giving no room to assess our own traumas and our own oppressors, New America pushed an agenda of neurological plasticity. In these mindsets, we understood our intentions—and that's it—because effect was irrelevant. After all, questioning the reasoning behind New American policy was a socially uncouth practice that New America had zero capacity for. Was it even criminalized to openly dissent? We didn't know, as select critique was lethal.

What we did know, however, was that open dissent within BioDome parameters was, perhaps, grounds for abduction.

In the beginning of the New American Regime, finding our own peace without the accountability or assistance of our oppressors felt strengthening, as if we could survive *anything*. And while this was true to an extent, I could see our reactions leading us to self-harm as much as they led us to great art. We were only human, and thus, we deserved both rage and frivolity.

With no further conversations, New American people were left gaslit and depleted, constantly questioning their own moral code as institutions were excused for their atrocities and workers were bereft of protections.

"You can't change people, you can only change yourself" was a motto New American counselors, therapists, and recovery groups held dear. However, in these moments of reclaiming my worth from the oppressors I'd let in, I would wonder, *Who gets to decide how I react? Had something been done that was so violent—so shameful—that my reactions were going to expose some truth?*

Exhausted with the respectable complacency of unaccountable, deadpan New America, I wanted to scream in the name of the Regime, my worst selves, and of Pluto.

Exiting Quakertown and navigating remote, unpaved terrain back east and toward Canada, I had a subtle rebirth. I didn't want to explain what I had learned at Demonixa's because I was here, in this van, and finally enjoying a ride with the people I loved in varied, often fractured ways.

It was now obvious that Fulanito and I sat next to one another every time we hit the road. I'd sit on the left, and Fulanito, on the right. And if Fulanito had agreed to drive, I called shotgun without shame as if it were math—the order of operation. I was a New Yorker; I luckily did not know how to drive, but was very skilled at reading maps.

Fulanito had this tuft of hair—a glorified devilock that swung over his left temple when he looked down to read. This was the image implanted in my head, the guilty pleasure of an awkward glance four to twelve hours a day, every day, until we made it home.

Every so often, he grabbed this piece of hair as if it had done something wrong, as if it were not supposed to be there but could not be removed. This tuft was not the same texture as the rest of his head, and maybe, because of that, he felt it should be destroyed or played with like a frayed joyride or a very tempting cigarette.

On occasion, he would glance over. I would glance back and squint my lower lash line toward the disarray of my furrowed brows, slurping on my frappé.

I was always slurping on a thick, frothy frozen latte full of caffeine, plants, and minerals that kept my guts and my mobility functional. I'd convince myself that I'd chosen this method of ingesting because it was the easiest to procure on the road. I loved this shake with its bits and pieces; sultry, overbearing chunks of unpressed maca root; and its very few additional flavors because I'd packed the perishables so poorly. It was absolutely alright, though, because I enjoyed this tension between me and my broken Achilles' heels—this performance of *slurping.*

As long as he and I were in this space of autonomy and incoherence, we could see the light beyond the draining cycles of eye tag. We could fuck around and find out how terrible we could be when no one was watching.

On unchartered terrain, I, unhinged, would unsuspectedly spill drops of maca frappé on my tits, over the distressed cotton and the seat belt.

FARTS
SUNSETS
AWKWARD
BONERS
ONLY THE
PROBL

Fulanito would aggressively pull his unkempt tuft with two fingers, then slide back up in strategic impulse, making sure he could feel every piece, every split end. As a finale, he would twirl it, a triple axel, a quad, and then a little more because it felt so fucking good.

I wiped my tits, trying ever so hard to not glance over.

In the body, there's a reservoir, or a control tower, between the pelvis and all exit points. It holds the memory of survival: what had survived, what had fractured, what parts were still healing, and what was to be avoided.

My foolproof method of trigger avoidance was easy as all hell: stay single, attend sex parties outside the community, and stay present—as in run errands in amazing outfits, get a cat who will outlive me, have a sick band that shreds, but most importantly, don't fucking fall in love.

Don't fucking surrender to the undeniable tug from their eyes as you scream together to all the songs that pour from your mouths like revolution. Don't cower when he looks to his right and you look to your left in an instant that feels eternal—as if there were no room for love in sex, drugs, and rock 'n' roll.

Despite it all, I preferred to surrender. A couple months ago, when the universe and Fulanito's subliminal mannerisms had started showing me the truth, it had felt like drugs, like that threshold between swallowing the pill and euphoria, that space where living could finally be understood.

Because, *well,* Fulanito definitely had a crush on me.

Okay? Carolina Tatiana San Lazaro De La Quinta, are you listening? Every morning and every night, I asked myself whether I was losing my mind or effectively reading between the lines before I pulled a tarot card, in order to understand the convoluted signals of a stoic poet with an earthbound heart space, protected by gold lamé bricks.

Hell if I knew how I was going to make it out of this one without my head in my ass and a rusty nail in my control tower, oxidizing the bitter ends of Pluto's last showdown and my last regret.

I wiped the last bit of sludge off my tits and reached for my canvas bag that always sat beneath my corner. My corner was the queen's lair, as whatever seat I chose to inhabit quickly acquired the vibe of a lost teen's bedroom but with thirty-some years of angst-ridden experience. Beneath color-coded Tupperwares full of nuts and hot chips sat a black-and-white zebra-print satchel that matched every additional item.

I intended to pull out blunt wraps, a bag of weed, a shaker of tajin, and sandalwood spray, but instead I saw Forever's gift that was slowly losing its intention beneath awkward silence and my own disbelief in transformation. I pulled it out and unraveled the red string that was lightly stitched across the red velvet box that carried three small plastic bags of Forever's murky, nebulous ritual.

"Hey, did I tell y'all about the gift Forever made me?" I widened my eyes in self-deprecating sarcasm because I was not sure how to walk in this power. I was finally investigating self-care outside of making art, outside of yelling about trauma and dancing for the revolution of Dystopia. I was now dancing for the revolution of my deeply hidden, stone-cold heart space.

If I were to walk in this alleged power, my crevice could become the energetic organ that pushed me to shit on Pluto's debris and bask in my new fire so it can burn, so I can mourn freely, so I can fuck freely, so I can rewrite my legacy, and die. I could bathe in the ashes of this decaying version of myself that was so powerful, so important, so sarcastic, hilarious, confusing, necessary, and so complete yet so outdated—a version of myself that had been left to the wolves of a bitter past but was, from now on, a beautiful memory of who I had been when I was broken.

Nothing will ever withstand all the art, all the revolutions, and all the fights I won while shitting on every last memory of Pluto. I wore trauma on my sleeve like a heroine—though a bitter one who was always trying to figure out the difference between *reactionary* and *resilient*.

"Wow, cool! I'm so proud of you, CT." Oracle was typically an aggro Virgo with a piercing Scorpio Rising, so her kindness and support was striking and reassuring, as if I had pleased my therapist once and for all. She exhibited the kind of support that tapped my spine. It was difficult for me to differentiate my bad ideas from brilliant risks, but Oracle seemed so grounded in her risk-taking, her choices. Her affirming hand was always a little shocking because she was my left arm, the one who saw the pit of fire before I walked straight into it. "What's in the mix?"

"I have no idea, other than flowers. Florecitas blancas like the ones I'm supposed to offer the abuelas at the next river we pass."

"Wow, she really put you on a regimen!" Reggy was investigating his own regimen, day and night, in his attempts to reclaim his postwar Appalachian harvest. His eagerness to prioritize the ancestral meaning of his medicine inspired me to do the same. "Noice."

Fulanito stared down at the dark ziplock bags of earth and spirit and then up to my face. His jaw dropped, and he had zero words. I looked back, and after a three-second delay, I offered a sudden flash of tongue, like a small, precious reptile in heat.

"Wow, I can smell that from here! It's lovely," Ganache said. He was driving and making sly judgments on tone while our new demo played on repeat. We loved his fuss-free, no-holds-barred way of being our dad.

I wanted a dad, even as I forgot that this whole wellness and healing trash pile of self-destruction had been handed to me long ago by a brilliant musician of a father who'd taken twenty-seven years to get back to me after I'd asked when he'd get home from his gig. Now we rest in ripe camaraderie, as he'd fled the USA many years ago.

I needed to find something beyond me wrecking my brain, my families, my homes, and my potentially gorgeous nights all because I was afraid that once the flesh became tender and the wounds were revealed, I would still want one thing and one thing only—cocaine, if not Fulanito.

Terrified, I officially wanted to shed my scales into this new, conceptual me. She would be better at speaking, but less funny and more boring. She would be so calm without the temptation to sabotage the gorgeous moments that felt *scary good*: the staring, the tongues, the breaths, the nasty and divine artful chaos of raw potential love. She would be the stoic mystery that I saw in Demonixa, in Oracle, and in the abuelas who had invented the cocimientos that kept us intact.

She would be divine. She would not be longing for cocaine, cock, ass, pussy, brains, stability, pleasure, fierce gowns, or cheap glitter—she would just have it in her uncanny holy spirit.

COMPERSION

We continued our trek to the northernmost points of east Dystopia, worlds that were wild and chaotic and beyond the American debris of Abaddon's destruction. The northern corridor of the region was Canadian Dystopia—old Toronto, Montreal, and Saskatchewan. Like New York, much of Canada had followed suit after the Regime's North American dissection in 2110, promising fair trade, Indigenous sovereignty from Alaska to Nova Scotia, and a widespread tact for wellness, if you will; the Regime, however, had lied through the skin of their teeth and the mercenaries in their tanks, clear-cutting national preserves one coercive nuclear pact after another.

New America had overthrown the shimmering, fragile democratic socialist utopia of the Bloom because the fascists were armed. The

Collective had been trustworthy and honorable in its efforts during the Bloom to remove the destructive potential of violent regimes, but in honor of the god-fucking Constitution, the right to privatized land had been maintained.

Amid the compassion of the Bloom, racist and misogynist vibes did not warrant a search of your private property, though the means for a random search warrant remained complex and outdated. Despite additional socialist frameworks of shared resources and their intersection with the economy, the Post-American Bloom persisted with their own initial promises.

And as usual, when any gifts to the undeserved were finally given—such promises were exploited.

During the socialist bloom, privatized land became shrouded and untapped. Beneath the topsoil, the mantle, and the fertile, sacred grounds, museums of nuclear assault rifles and rare tanks swelled. Silent offshore international pacts with neighboring war-ravaged regimes multiplied, setting a global precedent for the *New American* manifest destiny. Underground, among newborn pipelines and concealed masses of land tucked along the Navajo Nation, sat the seed of New America, back when it was still minimized as a simpleminded, lifeless threat to Make America Great Again.

2110 wasn't only the year of the North American dissection, but it was also the year Fulanito and I were sluts. Simpler times.

Fulanito was heavily spoken for then and had been married for five years, as Generation Hex wore their god-fearing cowardice and mammalian needs for partnership on their sleeves. However, during those years, the newlywed, newly polyamorous couple had painted the town red at underground sex clubs and at the monthly Cheap Glitter 4 Cheap Blowjobs Fundraisers 4 Harm Reduction. We called this our bloom, our blooming boners and elongated glances and Fulanito's bizarre attempt at polyamory that, in fact, did not include multiple lovers. It did not include connection or fucking around beyond the whirlwind orgies we collectively fell into from time to time at nightclubs. Fulanito's game was a trauma bond roulette of performative prowess, but most controversially—staring at me.

He would stare when I walked, when I spoke, and when I danced, peering from behind the stacks or DJ booth or other focal point like a night shift stagehand looking for love and trouble.

Fulanito stared for years, and I danced, laughed, or sneered back. Throughout the most dismal nights of his and Narnia's marriage, Fulanito would stare beyond the abyss of compersion while Narnia fucked her other partner, Oracle, on the dance floor. Digging her fingers into Oracle, Narnia would kiss her neck, and Oracle would moan, and Narnia would laugh and hoist Oracle up toward our sky, the rotating disco ball that lit our most vulnerable parts. Fulanito would then snap back into reality and raise a glass alongside the surrounding ring of voyeurs.

We'd stare as I clapped and celebrated our collective freedom—a reclamation of our worst lovers, our most unforgiving organs, and the undulating complexity of being queer and exhausted with our pride. Now, though, we mostly feel unrest.

We stared on our walks home and our reprieves from being renowned. We stared at dusk when we packed our gear onto the hatchback before every show. We stared during every drum fill and every climax of every word we wrote when things were softer and lonelier.

Playing live music was like fucking or masturbating in front of all your friends but without the sexuality—if you chose to keep your clothes on. The penetrable rhythmic pulse of coordination kept it mystical and intimate, while the freedom of loving the words you were singing and the notes you were playing kept it climactic and embodying.

Before the evolution of the colonized mind and body, sensuality was about our carnal movement. On the best nights, a song could easily become a full-body awakening, a prophecy, an orgasm. We screamed our stories and destroyed our tools for a sensory overload because our pleasure was not a threat but a sacred gift. And during Cheap Glitter's electrifying pulse of synchronized breathing and yelling and noodling and blasting, Fulanito and I kept staring.

We stared when we packed up and set out and headed back to sleep. We stared in our dreams. We stared the morning after our crusades on warm concrete porches in alien towns with bloody fingertips and doe-eyed wanderlust.

We stared on video calls during awkward band meetings where we'd get nothing done, nothing settled, and nothing advanced aside from the knowledge that maybe there was more to this *staring*.

Being single is not for the weak, for the traumatized, for the despairing. I can attest to this as a weak, traumatized, single woman in despair.

I didn't *feel* an end to New America, nor the tempered heartstrings between Fulanito's emotional unavailability and my nuanced freedom. And so, we sat in them, tying them in gorgeous, complex overhand knots while we laughed about death and destruction. We wrapped them around our joints for cushion because we had so much left to learn about grieving our worst lovers. This helped us stay reactionary—fighting, singing, shredding, staring—but not fucking. Heavens, not fucking.

Driving into Canada, we hit a sharp swerve against a wall of Sheetrock, and my maca frappé went flying into the earth. Fulanito extended his arm over me to rescue my thermos from its death and handed it to me.

"Oh my god! You're my hero," I said, with furrowed brows and the underlying sense of resurrection.

Reggy often kept to himself in the room he'd built in the back of the van for him and Smarties, his late, great mastiff. It was now our lab, our biodiesel garage, our wellness retreat, and a hydroponic garden that kept us fed. We hardly entered since Reggy had painstakingly designed its architecture and function to sustain his and Ganache's maintenance routines, and we didn't want to disrupt his secret opus. Reggy seemed tired of the whirlwind and checked out of my chaos, but his purpose kept him unphased.

As my late-night cheesecake, we had run the ups and downs of torrid love with anecdotes and ideas, but before my eyes, Reggy was tapping into a solution.

"Hey y'all, did you see what I did?" Reggy peeked from the lab doors. We all checked our phones, wholly familiar with his knack for exposing his own chaos through passive aggressive memes or heartfelt subliminal song lyrics. Reggy had posted a very forward-facing truth: a photo of him and Gemmx with a caption that read "finally."

Gemmx's comment exhibited requited truth: "srsly."

"Reggy! You did it!" Oracle yelled, and we collectively gasped for air.

"I realized a two-page confession of love wasn't necessary. I think they're going to be in Montreal!"

"Cute! So, we'll both have dates in Canada?" Oracle had her own Canadian love story, and the two smiled.

"Hell yeah. Only one life to live or destroy." Reggy shuffled back to the lab. We all laughed, except Fulanito, who bore the brunt of reading between the lines. My laughter trailed off when I caught his silence. I

EARTH
MENSTRUA
OCEAN

looked over, and he did too, catching sight of each other's puckered lips, furrowed brows, and longing.

On occasion, Reggy's hydroponic avocado harvest would be brimming with fruit, so we had to eat them faster than normal.

"Does anyone want an avocado?" Fulanito didn't wait for an answer and crouched into the lab through the arched doorway.

"What the fart? Who is she?" he asked Reggy in shock and awe.

"A jade tree." Reggy was tending to his latest harvest. "It started with a clipping from back home." He spun his creation beneath the purple glow.

"How the hell did this get so big in the last forty-eight hours?" Fulanito squealed at a stone-faced Reggy.

"By singing to them." Reggy was stealth and precolonial in both his knowledge and his practice. ". . . and menstrual blood." He didn't smile and returned to his pruning.

"Wow. You're legendary." Fulanito stared into the abyss of the knotted branches and overgrown leaves of jade. In love with nature, but not so much biology, he preferred to eat plants and pass out in them rather than understand what they needed. Reggy returned to Fulanito's gaze with a single raised brow and a cocky smirk.

"Why thanks, buddy."

Old Montreal was another minefield of despair and violence, scattered with pockets of resilient people haphazardly doing their best. So, we stuck to our cesspools: punk rock shows and convergent spaces dedicated to the resistance.

A few more miles passed, and we stopped to refuel.

"Bienvenue à Montréal!" The biodiesel guy was jolly and hospitable—I wanted to be him. "What you kids are doin' is awesome! Keep it up!" Rather, I wanted to see myself as he saw me.

Contrary to speculation, we enjoyed these moments when we got to sit in our self-righteous, self-soothing, and self-congratulatory reprieve.

Tonight will be amazing, I repeated to myself in a tired mantra I chose to believe every time I remembered the infinity of grieving.

We reached old Montreal at the peak of dawn and enjoyed a sprawling orange sunrise. If Dystopia had done anything, it had blurred state lines and the bureaucratic dots between continents. We drove into town and felt at home in Montreal's reclaimed urban environment that was half dilapidated and half thriving in their own bones and armor made up of string lights, city lights, local art, red lights, neon lights, families, and vendors. It was strategic survival with a town hall that peculiarly gave a shit.

We pulled up to our lodging on boulevard Saint-Laurent, above an abandoned bank with pillars like the Regime's, but ones that were worn and weathered. Boulevard Saint-Laurent was a once overwhelming downtown that had become subtle and pure. Half asleep and half awake, everyone except Fulanito and I ran up to their rooms as if they had just won some battle or pissed off some gatekeeper.

"Hey! CT, wanna smoke this joint with me?" Fulanito spoke to me, and I looked down at the fresh joint rolled in strawberry papers that matched the merriment of his hot pink curls. I smiled back. That meant yes.

"Do you ever just have no idea how to make a full sentence, so you like, do all kinds of stupid reactionary shit 'cause it's all you've ever been expected to do?" Fulanito exhaled and unfurled his can of worms. "Like, no one had taught you better?"

"Hmm. Yes, but I'm full of sentences—to a fault." I smiled and ashed the strawberry joint onto the steps, shuffling the dust beneath my sandal and inching closer to Fulanito's bare feet. "I'm kind of obsessed with articulating everything for everyone because it's all I knw how to do.

That was my role, holding my family together and making them talk about shit. I think it makes me kind of annoying."

"Well, maybe you can help me if it gets weird?"

"Oh, yeah?"

Fulanito looked into my eyes and paused, like maybe this, in fact, was the end of the world. But it was okay. It was the end of everything I had ever known and everything I had ever unlearned. In my eyes, he was light—motivation to do Demonixa's spell and drink the potions and do the ritual and honor the wisdom that I'd been resisting because it's *beyond* wisdom but a newfangled open wound. I let out a breath and smiled.

"Mm-hmm." Our lips were the closest they had ever been.

Fulanito smiled closer, and I blushed, looking downward at the curdling strawberry joint, then looking up.

"We should go to bed." Fulanito pulled back. "We're playing Canada tomorrow!"

"Yeah, totally. Canada, another country." We snickered. I did not move my eyes away from his. I was exhausted with anything that wasn't the awkward truth. Maybe we wouldn't kiss, but I would continue to stare into his abyss as if it were in there that I would find what I had always been looking for.

I woke up ecstatic. I opened my hellfire phone, messaged Reggy and Oracle, and said three Hail Marys.

CT: YALL. FULANITO AND I HAD A MOMENT.

Reggy: Fucking jesus its 7AM

Oracle: Cool! Maybe you should tell him how you feel? Since we're all bandmates?

CT: *eye roll emoji*

Oracle: btw Im up now—wanna roll me a J and meet me on the porch?

CT: Fuck YEA.

Reggy: Can you all please text on a separate thread? I just drove us down a dirt path on a mountain for 3 hours while we got chased by goats. yOUrE WELcoMeee. GOODMoRRNING.

CT: OMG REG WHY DO YOUR TEXTS MAKE SOUNDS??????

Oracle: Damn, left on read. 20 minutessss?!

To kill twenty minutes, I regressed into my nylon sleeping bag, silk pillowcases, and neon green vibrator shaped like some kind of space dick. My masturbation practice had started feeling like a cyclical state of purgatory: the same sleazy rock playlist, the same moment in fabricated time when I'm making out with my ultimate crush, who's unfortunately also my bandmate, on a circular velvet bed while all our friends sit around enjoying the evening as if it were any other. We're all turning full face, frocks, and plumage. Suddenly, Fulanito grabs my shoulders from behind and begins to kiss the back of my neck. Squeezing the despair out of me through a plunged neckline, Fulanito pushes his hands down my tits and toward my trail while his dick effortlessly thrusts against the soft plateau below my asshole. With two fingers, he massages my labia against my clit, and to my pleasant surprise, begins to fuck me from behind, all to the wailing rock 'n' roll classics of 2069—the year of the revolution—and I am breathless.

Eventually, we nonchalantly break to contribute to the conversation as he innocently plays with my nipple. Whatever—it's *just fashion*.

Ah. The good life. Partnership. The security of knowing who you will fuck at the party. Well, at least I have loneliness and trauma and something to write about and compare to the looming apocalypse that my generation was forced to desensitize itself to—*goddammit.*

Fuck love, anyway, I'd often think after having an orgasm by myself. Because nothing can *possibly* be as exciting as making myself cum by sitting on a barstool with my legs crossed while I gingerly enjoyed whatever music was playing whether I liked it or not. This was easy after a double Kahlua Malibu. You know, a cafecito for lonely bitches.

Twenty minutes had not yet passed. I took a pause to reflect on the lighter side of apocalyptic despair and remembered last night.

LESBIANS

They called us Generation Hex because we were wounded and unwilling to put faith, trust, or investment in these broken systems that had very little to show for themselves. However, we had our ancestors, our grit, and our histories. We had our minds and our art and the goal to elevate everything that global assimilation had erased. We created alternate worlds and made art with our wounds because, after all, in such a comfy state of fascist, neoliberal white supremacy, who even fucking wanted the approval of such a soul-sucking mainstream? Like, who cared that the government was another collective, except that this one was run by a goddamn robot who swore it wanted to abolish human labor? Abolishing our skill and our autonomy didn't count as liberation; neither did abolishing oxygen, regenerative wildlife, stem cell research, windmills, and solar panels. So, we just sulked, navigating sinkholes and mudslides and the glorious disarray of our beloved Dystopia. We'd managed and found purpose in a self-sufficient minefield—the oligarchy could have their sheep placenta facials.

Democratic fascists loved fracking as much as they loved a good facial. They would say it was for sustainability, but it was actually for profit—accelerated sustainability for tired centrists who wouldn't know revolution if it was snuck into their latte by the ghost of Che Guevara.

They called it symbiosis—I called it violation. Personally, I would have loved to have lived during generation of Democratic Socialism, but we were the last generation: the generation that broke the silence, the generation that pulled the apple from the tree because it tasted good, the generation called Hex because, apparently, we had hexed the planet.

I identified with all Gen Hex stereotypes because we were like Generation X, that turn-of-the-twentieth-century generation that had fabricated subcultures about pain and suffering and creating your own world because the state was genuinely uninterested. Like them, we chose to isolate ourselves, and instead of fixing our wounds and reclaiming the mass media, we fostered the *alternative* and made art about how sad we were because it was the end of the fucking world, right?

At least, that was how Abuela Amparo had made being a bisexual artist in the 1990s sound, according to La Otra's lyrics. I come from a long line of angry women, and I can assure you—great art can cancel great pain.

Healing is for pussies . . . I often thought to myself while I scratched my pussy and wondered where I'd gone wrong. I sat cross-legged on the porch, begging my brain to not dip back into the last time I'd sat here, inches from what had felt like intimacy.

"Sure, yeah, I mean, I've got the PTSD, but I just want to be held," I moaned to Oracle. "I want the perfect stranger that is the next love of my life to—"

"I hear ya, man. But isn't that, like, what we're told is the answer to happiness? So, we gotta find something better."

"Sure. But what if we don't find it in us to, like, love ourselves? Like all these baby queers with their revolutionary hope? I'm just so tired."

"Amen to that." Oracle sealed our despair. We slurped on our lavender lattes in an attempt to believe in a purpose that, for me, felt empty without a better half. "Except I figured out polyamory! Bada boom!"

"Womp, womp. I guess I don't mind being such a fucking mammal." In an attempt to rip the Band-Aid off and love myself, I considered the notion of lasting bonds. Lasting sch-lasting. That's what my therapist had told me to do—talk all night to the ghosts who stopped by with reminders of their haters, abusers, legacies, and torrid balance beams. I was supposed to listen to the ones who took me seriously and shatter the ones who ridiculed my disparity.

Self-love was always thrown around in quirky anecdotes and fun slogans like trash after a good party. Happiness was not simple. Taking my own and everyone else's advice while trying to be the person who "did the work" was strange and uncomfortable. I regularly looked back at days I "should" have enjoyed with regret and longing that transmutes into shame, so I searched for the essential light at the end of that day: a song, a lesson, a heartbeat.

Cheap Glitter was the love child of my incandescent turmoil, so I forgave it regularly.

When empires fall, they take the people down with them—whether we liked it or not—and that hurt the most, the fact that we couldn't converge with the weather or the ether in order to save our communities

MPOST
TOTA

and heal the earth from global fascism. So, we did what we could and then yelled as our ancestors had into the same ether, into the oceans, into the systemic turbulence, and into the planets that would devour us and synthesize us and attempt to keep us whole. Our fits of rage were sacred, for they sustained our subtle communion with a decaying Earth.

Cheap Glitter was the force teenage me never could have imagined. And because the system's failures were a deadly cycle, they could only be interrupted by giving a shit about our role in justice, by the smell of our van, by the frays on our clothes, and by the swerving dissent in the veins on our tendons. Our role was not to dismantle this from the inside. It was to scream from sacred underworlds where we had less governance and more control.

Oracle, however, thrived in the axis of our underworld and the dominant culture. Her professional training in therapy and psychology gave her the numbing power to hold space for our bullshit. She was a Virgo and was able to normalize and see the pragmatism in the whirlwind of ideas tossed around by me, a Gemini with heavy Cancer placements. We were proud to make music with her, and we knew she was making her mother proud as her spirit watched us and held her so she could hold the incompetent lovelorn messes that were her bandmates—or that, at least, were Fulanito and I.

Reggy was also a Virgo. He knew disgruntled romance as I did, but he did not know romanticizing a mess. He knew about tending to curiosity and being strategic about preserving our personal power. I did not have time for curiosity, just for acting on unripe initiatives. Reggy was thoughtful in his deliveries, though, so I always took notes. He wanted to give room to the looming deaths, complex dynamics, and the new sort of space we would all initially need to make dynamic changes tangible.

Fulanito had a lot of earth in his chart, and I had a lot of water with a fiery Venus. Together, we just wanted to fan the flames, fuck around, and find out—albeit in a beautiful home with exciting upholstery.

Oracle was *not* having this situationship, this intangible web of obsession and unspoken heartstrings that ruled my life, kept Fulanito sending me crumbs, and kept me smiling back through lyrical Morse code and secret tongue. So, I tried to be the best front woman, booker, designer, and songwriter anyone had ever known for the mere price of my emotional instability and an uncomfortable comedic hell for the entertainment of all who loved trash TV.

Oracle licked the exterior of her blunt wrapper as she was midway through a smoke.

"I just felt so dirty stalking his social media and overanalyzing how he flirts with everyone when I detach," I confessed to Oracle. "I mean, in public, he ignores me *all* the time aside from staring at me from the other side of the room, right? I want to die."

Oracle nodded in agreement, and I took a drag off the soft, raw tobacco that held a thick line of cannabis.

"I mean, no, I want to live," I countered.

"Oh god, C. We *all* do that!" Oracle said without hesitation or embarrassment. "Who fucking cares! 'Social media stalk until they talk' is what I say—the world is ending. Fuck it."

"So, that makes it okay?" The longer I went trusting my gut without "checking" on it, the more I knew I was healing old wounds. I wanted to sit there, intuitive and at peace, sober and not an internet stalker.

Unfortunately, healing was expensive and inaccessible in New America. The long weeks of lines for craniosacral therapy appointments only made the comedy and artfulness of self-sabotage too marketable and relatable in this apocalypse. And so, there we were, mortal humans lacking in the divine abilities of intuition and telepathy that our late twenty-first century ancestors had known too well. We made up for it by shameless stalking.

"So, what did you find?

"Oh nothing . . . I mean, sure: slime stuff, deep memes and classic rock, some hot femmes. You know, the same as us," I confessed. "I got this reading once, long before tour, about giving him the space to grieve his own trauma while trusting in what brings me joy." I took a larger drag. "Fuli was so shamed and degraded back in the day. Every moment of prowess is such a breakthrough. I don't want to suck his life out." I sighed. "I'm trying to obey the tarot cards and hone my *alleged power . . .*"

"Good for you!" Oracle sustained me. "Doesn't change that he's totally weird around your alleged power. Sounds like it's time to shut up or make out so you don't sabotage our band!" Oracle snatched the joint from my hand and looked at me with jest and exhaustion. Oracle was an oracle—a prophecy.

I was sick of excusing my own human error. I wanted to turn my feelings into great works of art, not great lapses of time lost to obsession and hidden from Fulanito, the culprit of my discomfort and the curator of the sweet subliminal nothings. He was the instigator of the discreet back-seat footsies that kept me warm and deluded at night.

I did not hate social media. I loved seeing our achievements and our outfits, but seeing our insecurities and shame spirals spilling into reactionary responses to what we saw as opposed to what we knew? Not so much.

"I'm quitting social media, actually." I recoiled into my inner goody two-shoes that rattled the warrior in all of us. "I have to be divine."

"You don't have to be so hard on yourself." Oracle was not amused.

“Why don’t you take Forever’s advice?” Oracle took a puff and blew it onto my face. “Do her spell! See what’s in there.”

“What about maybe just some acid?” We laughed. “What about your problems? Did you make out last night??”

“They’re the same. And yes!” Oracle was grieving like the rest of us, but she also had an undying commitment to our host, Barnaby Blacklist.

Oracle held my shoulders and swayed me from side to side. She reached toward the small speakers by the ashtray, put on something out of 2099, and asked me to dance.

“Sometimes you just have to put on some classic rock!” she said.

I danced and dreamed of avoiding the drugs, the lines, the mistakes, and the false attempts at elevating my consciousness with chemical cocktails of uppers and downers that eventually made me depressed.

We danced. We did not mind that time was not on our side, because when we danced, we found peace. Mid-twirl, Barnaby Blacklist peeked at us from the front door and called us in for breakfast.

Everyone gathered in the kitchen. Barnaby was a wild magician with a strange swerve in her fringe, like some kind of wizard girl from another planet. Undoubtedly, Barnaby’s grandmother had traveled to Montreal from an off-grid land project in Ladakh, India, and it showed. Barnaby had floating magnetic structures placed throughout the house, all representative of some kind of healing process—like altars. However, this was ancestral magic that I had not heard of, as these ancestors worked with gravitational pull like mine did with the ocean.

Oracle and Barnaby went way back, having been star-crossed lovers during the shift to the Regime. They had met in school in New York during the Bloom, both studying the intersections between sound engineering, American Sign Language, and revolutionary audio. Barnaby had left old New York when the Regime began its pillage and had reconnected to her roots in old Montreal in order to build something in the dilapidated space that was her home.

I loved to watch what I secretly called *normal* love. Barnaby and Oracle could comfortably shift focus given space and circumstance—their connection was true; it may even *be* love.

Barnaby and Oracle embodied calm in their kiss and in the way they held hands to catch up. They were lesbians—a lifestyle I was secretly jealous of. Bisexuality always left me winded and frazzled because it was not always a holistic coven of ethical affection. I always seemed to have one hand in the queer resistance and the other leading a discourse at the nightclub on the complexities of competition, gender roles, and trying to fuck some garage rock dude. Lesbians were so fucking cool with their convictions and their ability to elevate feminist resilience over lovelorn drama—or maybe it was just because the grass was always greener on the other side.

I guess I would never know, sulking there and trying to decode the secret language of trauma through subliminal sweet nothings and ancestral witchcraft. I mean, don't get me wrong, I was having a super fun time being sexually attracted to the general human species, never landing on anyone's desired range on the gender spectrum, and enduring a death cycle of sexual tension. I just would have preferred that Fulanito Del Mar kiss me or marry me with the accelerated bliss of the traditional lesbian trajectory than whatever it was that we were doing.

I would know. I had gone through many whirlwind sapphic romances that had begun in an instant honeymoon and ended with a hangover after forty-eight hours of sobriety.

Barnaby and Oracle were professional lesbians, and by that I meant emotionally mature. They exhibited the kind of serene assurance my scrubby heroism wanted to feel and see in the world. They were an inspiration, and Fulanito and I watched and took notes while we drank rosé and enjoyed fennel and heirloom tomato salad with a Cajun-spiced Chilean sea bass—like life was once again gay and normal.

Reggy and Ganache were sulking in a strange, advanced memory foam love seat with the look and feel of a one-hundred-and-fifty-year-old waterbed. They laughed and poured one another elderberry-infused seltzers in floral demitasse cups.

Fulanito picked French fries from my plate, and I retracted them with my mouth, simultaneously annoying and delighting the ring of mature, emotionally available queers.

I felt feral with Fulanito, unhinged at the sights of passion and hunger. We were animals together—and I liked it.

MODERN THERAPY

I didn't know whether it was this ticking trauma bomb that kept me feeling ugly or whether Fulanito was actually an atypical fuckboy, straight out of the books that'd been written by my great-grandmother's generation. I didn't know, so I sulked. I invited a psychic to our old Montreal show in exchange for hits of pot or housing. I received the validation of mutual attraction but continued to cry.

Apocalypse was suddenly not enough of a reason for twin souls to coalesce in spite of our own unwoven issues. Knowing was not enough. Accepting that we couldn't control one another, I considered alternate routes to resilience and opening Forever's concoction.

We arrived at the venue with carts of gear and no vehicle to honor the carbon-free ordinance that happened after midnight. That night was not like most nights when I was avoiding the well of exhaustion that was a result of either the overactive joy or poison of love—I forget. Because for now, I could just *not believe* it.

Everyone was in love with Fulanito, and today, it was particularly electrifying. For tonight's performance, I'd forged barbed-wire boundaries around my heart. Naturally, we could both find our individual peace—we often didn't have a choice. Fulanito found whirlwind homes in screaming fans, fawning witches, and ethereal connections to wounded, displaced queers. I found purpose and peace in crying fans and brown girls with purple hair reclaiming the things they'd lost to terrible love. However, peace would bare its thorns when we wanted love instead.

I walked onto the stage and grabbed the mic to scream in return.

"HEY EVERYBODY! I HOPE YOU DON'T MIND, I THINK I HATE MYSELF TONIGHT!" As I sang, Oracle accented my cry for help with an audible threat of survival. The song began, an anthem for casual self-loathing, and the crowd united with benediction, though not in an alarming way. We thrived in Dystopia as long as the destruction of the world was a means not to an end but to art and communion in disparity.

I, however, had only this moment—this song—to dispel my wounded insecurities. The rest of the night, however, would be for my typical donning of a self-righteous feminist hero's mask. Just for tonight, I begged for anonymity and forgiveness.

Earlier, I had cried in the greenroom, at the schmooze fest, in Oracle's arms, on Reggy's bass guitar, in front of Fulanito, and in front of the hordes of onlookers who often romanticized my pain. I cried on a long walk with a joint that took me three bands' sets to finish, causing me to arrive late for our own set. I cried onstage, backstage, and exiting my post. The masses rejoiced.

Everyone seemed to love us—so why could I not love me? Why could I not love this far-fetched ideal of being in a *beloved* rock band? This reality, as a prospect, had kept me alive twenty years ago when Cheap Glitter was a realistic pipe dream because the sky was the limit then. *So what if our band never worked out?* I'd have thought. *Who cared?* It would've been okay because the sky was so vast, so close, so proud with abundance and resilience and the stories of our ancestors who'd taught us that purpose was Phoenician and that the earth was salvageable. It could fall and rise cyclically because when we loved our earth, its resources became endless.

Now, we rationed resources and valued knowledge. We had no alternate plans, no plan-B food truck, wellness center, letterpress company, or animal rescue—no funding from the government to follow those other dreams because the crazy one had not worked out. This lack of options was something we, Generation Hex, had grown up believing as angry teens with wide eyes for revolution and an eagerness to make our ideology global. We'd taken purpose for granted. So now I sat there on the curb of one of the best shows we had played away from home, rummaging in a well of fulfilled dreams that I didn't feel entitled to.

I exited the greenroom and walked aimlessly through the drenched bodies and fervent enthusiasm inspired by songs I'd written in my room with no net, just stark vulnerability. I walked, estranged from myself, with my hands in my pockets and my eyes directed at the fluorescents. I wondered who could tell I was hurting, who was planning my cancellation, and who was planning my intervention. I reached my band and forced stylish resilience.

"Hey, y'all. Sick set," Fulanito said to us in a cerebral tone that could either indicate detachment or focus. The mystery of Fulanito was both my Achilles' heel and my sanctuary. I was loud and obnoxious in practice; he was loud and obnoxious in theory.

While I watched us try to be normal after a glowing set, I dissected the unwarranted barbed wire surrounding our hearts and genitals. Maybe Fulanito wasn't the student of fuckboy patriarchy that I thought he was when I was drunk and thought everyone looked hotter, cooler, and better than me, when everyone looked fabulous and intact and aware of their worth and I was the untouchable ogre questioning my own.

Projecting my worst moments of manipulation, I asked myself aloud, "What am I going to choose to see: Fulanito engaging with a beautiful world full of resilient love or a red flag that never stopped to learn from the women he had hurt?"

Trust required confidence and engagement with the emptiest parts of my soul and the most sacred parts of falling in love.

"Hey, wanna go for a smoke?" Fulanito grabbed my wrist with the tips of his fingers and his third eye.

"Always." I stepped off my spiral. "I just don't want to be a weirdo. I obviously feel some kind of way." We walked, and I spit my truth with enough vagueness that wouldn't disrupt our prerogative.

"The other night, when I said I probably wouldn't be playing music if it wasn't for you . . ." Fulanito unraveled. "I really meant it!"

Fulanito hid behind his collar as he did when his vulnerability spilled into view. We continued to walk without many words, and my despair waned to the dismay of modern therapy. I was now at peace. I had validation beyond psychics and long stares. Actions spoke louder than words, and finding our own closure was successful feminism. Still, words can build expedited, everlasting foundations.

We arrived back at the venue, and I kept quiet watching everyone talk and connect. For the first time in what felt like my entire life, I watched love purposefully. I wanted him to engage with life, bodies, and smiles, and it was infectious. I watched in awe and dispersed into my own schmoozing, sinking into a hormonal balance that sang like hummingbirds and clicking glass.

Fulanito and I gathered around the debris of our performance, coiling cables and packing instruments. We were worn, reeking of moss and sweat. He looked at me as if I were a sprawling sunset, a boundless landscape, a work of art.

Oracle, Barnaby, Ganache, Reggy, and a stowaway Gemmx surrounded us. Evading their smirks and intoxicated with tense sensation, I tried to control my knowing smile.

Gemmx had evidently traveled to Toronto, hitching a ride on service transit like hoverships and electric freight trains. Reggy was like me: bewildered by affection yet anticipating extremes. Gemmx was extremely interested.

"So, did you guys have a cool walk?" Reggy asked us as if we were hot T and a source of joy, not another minefield.

"It was fucking awesome," Fulanito exclaimed, and I unfurled from my sexless misery.

"Yeah, it was." I self-actualized and returned to earth. "We even found these really cool gluten-free ice-cream cones in the trash, but no ice cream, thankfully, since it would have been gross. There weren't any wipes or anything. Whatever, it was normal." I looked up and saw that Fulanito had paused and was, in rare form, staring at me in public. Or maybe time had stopped? I couldn't tell.

My innards were warm, but my face was trained to stay poised at the first sight of love. After all, the space where we could lose ourselves in the stupid things that allowed us to laugh or smile was where we found home.

The climactic embodiment from feeling so alive transformed my body into a sanctuary. As opposed to the exhaustion from a lifetime of learning experiences, I could tell these new moments apart from the way I settled into my clothes and my shoes and the way my nerves fluttered like electricity.

We regained our wits and packed up. Everyone always asked why we packed our own gear and cleansed our own aftermath after both dream shows and shit shows. It was so difficult, in this day and age, to explain that being internationally renowned did not mean internationally well-equipped. Regardless, this labor of love and solitude always led us home amid the semblance of punk and the warfare of notoriety.

We returned to Barnaby's late that night. The sky was awash with the year's first nebula, and the galaxy was visible, as it often was in old Montreal when the city called for an intentional blackout.

"Hey, wanna go for a walk in the blackout?" Fulanito took my hand before I could answer, and we ran toward the fog-ridden Montreal streets, sneaking along fire pits and brick carcasses of empty rooms. We walked and spat onto the scattered puddles of radioactive debris so we could listen to the electric cackle.

We found an overlook to the side of an old refinery and gazed into the Milky Way. The night was clear, and Fulanito's smile looked crooked and tired beneath the glow of a blood moon that was half colonized, half livid, and curating retaliation.

Every time I, breathless or aroused, walked next to him, I would forget the collapse, the resistance, the everlasting war between the Regime and the earth, and I would only remember my will to live. And I'm not sure what my abuelas would say—in their autonomous glory—about this, but it was the kind of love that I was willing to suffer for.

"Hey, hold my arm." Fulanito's commanding softness wrecked me until I could no longer speak, only nuzzle my laughter into the damp upholstery of his stolen coat. We traversed the toxic hellscapes still twinkling with signs of life. Through the windows and beyond the architecture were candlelit families laughing, kids playing, couples fighting, people crying, people fucking, and people thinking tirelessly while smoking a cigarette that'd been lit by a tiny bonfire that might just last forever.

Fulanito was not much taller than me, so his eyes landed at the peak position when we talked and when I jumped, laughed, or flirted with my whole body. We were always so close to screaming or kissing. His hair was rough and tangled and Day-Glo magenta with the occasional disarray of city sludge. He liked to act as if everything were so simple. Fulanito was mostly raised by his father, until he fled at the dawn of the Regime. His father was a rawhide-clad forest guy who talked to trees, whistled with the wind, and carried on with his ancestral knowledge, part Inca, part Mediterranean. His father, Paolo, was still living and working as a land defender in an undisclosed tree sit, occasionally emailing Fulanito photos, anecdotes, and very few updates in compliance with the criminalization of dissent, the United States Post Office, and public transit. Thus, Fulanito had very little patience for despair. He was also a forest guy, a NorKal hippie, to a lowly Caribbean girl with no background in stillness but an eagerness to learn.

We walked back toward Barnaby's porch. Regrouping, my knees trembled, and my sacral void shook as if, maybe, I had just healed something.

Montreal was lit up with stars and constellations and the last bit of nature we could carry beside us in Dystopia. There was a chance I wouldn't want to drink tonight, as this piercing glow from Fulanito's

skin next to mine was blessing me with the secret to truly forgetting.

Entering Barnaby's home after midnight, we found the living room and circled a glowing sanctuary of collective heartstrings.

Oracle sat on a disheveled pile of knitted throws with Barnaby, laughing into the atmosphere. Ganache, in orchid long johns and noise-canceling headphones, perched on the balcony beneath the star-studded glow, talking to someone that made him smile. Reggy had brought Gemmx home and was slipping into a mutual, tender stupor beside the cackling fire.

I sat beside my own stupor: Fulanito and his unwoven desire.

Bisabuela Amparo had come of age during the time of Xeroxed fanzines, sexual taboo, and the hole in the ozone layer. Abuela Ulta was a millennial. They'd both played in bands who had never made it big but, rather, had made big strides for their communities and for the revolution. Their legacy was the reason I did what I did. They were the ancestors who screamed the loudest when my head got lost in my ass. My Mamá was a soft balm on my history of rage. An ER nurse, a vegetarian, and a homebody, she worried about me and about tour but ignored the internet to cope. When we spoke, she reminded me of the laws of nature—suffer, regenerate, live beautifully. Amparo never married; Ulta was in love, but once he strayed after Mamá's birth, she did not find love again. My mother, however, loved my father, scoffed at his exit, and found lovers at every port, sometimes cosmic or destructive, yet always a lesson or a story. She'd been born into this gorgeous revolution that allowed her to paint about joy and work for humanity. Her language was color and meditation. Some might say she was detached to a fault—I would say detached for a reason. I had learned my mother's will to live, albeit obsessed with breaking our generational curses.

ARM THE DOLLZ

My abuelas, ill-tempered by the corruption they'd been born into, warned me in dreams, in coffee grains, in cowrie shells, and in prophecies that made me half sick and half elated.

"Yes, Carolina, punk rock saved you too," Amparo would often whisper while Ulta laughed in the background. "But I don't know how love will keep you available for la revolución if you can't destroy your inner demons *before* you get a boyfriend."

"Ay vamos, abuelitas," I'd say to myself before a risk or a regret. "Cálmate los nervios, que I'm a big girl."

I followed Fulanito into Barnaby's attic, where accommodations were shared with warbling metallic pigeons, dimly lit fireflies, and the light of the moon. The window was circular, a portal to our next life or, at least, peace. Fulanito set our sleeping bags beside one another in an empty crevice facing east.

"This way, you can wake up to the sunrise." He knew me best, showing it without remorse. "Everything always makes more sense during the sunrise." We lay in our respective sleeping bags. I faced the window, and he faced me. "Goodnight, C."

"Goodnight." I smiled and pretended to sleep.

The morning after, the sun peeked above the dense purple horizon. Fulanito slept, curled into a nylon sleeping bag that had lost its form overnight. I was assured—eyes wide, staring at the light, and at peace—knowing I was stronger than my trauma. When I stepped into the kitchen, I would be a warrior representing truth, justice, and free expression. In the attic, however, I was human. My innards felt compressed with monarch butterflies that were violently swerving between my lungs and my pussy, grappling my large intestine, and screaming "Oh, my fucking heart!" as the fireflies watched and stared.

These Canadian fireflies were something else. Fulanito wiped the sleep off his jawline.

"Mornin', C." Fulanito smiled.

"Hey you." In silence, half naked and half asleep, we stretched, grunted, and gathered our things.

Downstairs, Barnaby packed us a basket of assorted granolas and rare fruit. We bid her farewell and began our drive back home to old New York.

PART 3

A LOVE SONG

TAMALES, MILK, AND ROSES

Riding in the van, en route to New York, I closed my eyes and thought about Amparo making coquito when I'd been too young to drink. My tía had knocked the cup out of her hands before we'd all burst into timeless laughter—a core memory.

I thought about my family communing with the coastal retreat our ancestors had begged for when they'd migrated from their homelands. Their homes had been fields of corn that told ancient stories; stone pyramids that refused to diminish; ripe plátanos, mangos, and tobacco leaves that were left as offerings at every door; and three different types of tamales at every holiday. I sunk in my memories and remembered what it had felt like to be raised in a world that willingly set our bodies free.

"I can't believe this tour is almost over. I don't think I'm ready to go back." Reggy sat up and looked into the distressed strands of pink and gold, glowing behind what was leftover of today's blue, both colors only visible from the Atlantic coast. "I just want to fucking cry," he added.

"I always remind myself that my ancestors lived hard and true—enough to leave us full. The fullness regenerates when the fun is over," I said as I tried to de-emphasize our grievances and make peace with uncertainty.

"True." Fulanito was a person of small words. "If we hadn't done this tour—who else would have?"

Ganache resurrected from a deep sleep. "U2, obviously."

We all laughed. U2 was an eccentric institution that had evolved into a postmortem AI once the Regime had taken control of the Vegas Sphere. We were lucky to be without red tape and full of purpose, so it was our responsibility to seal disparity with cynicism and joy. As wild ones with nothing to lose, it was our job to make sure we didn't get lost in a tragic mindset before our show. It was our job to derail the conversation into senseless territory so we could breathe longer and sing louder.

In a sea of passing laughs and gasses, I made an executive decision as a front woman.

I wasn't going to rock the boat and sabotage my band by falling in love with my bandmate who just happened to be the fucking ultimate queen of East Dystopia. I was going to persevere and be a rock and hold my heart against my sleeve when I sang and lock my heart away at night when our weakest parts thrived.

I was a top at life because nobody was going to hold me anyway. So, I might as well become an artisan and my own boss, right? Manage my every endeavor? Do everything for everyone, from making sandwiches to spreadsheets, without batting a lash because I couldn't care whether it was trust issues, passion, or systemic misogyny and racism. Goddammit, I had to do the fucking thing.

When the crickets sang and the sprawling sunsets faded, we were still in Dystopia, wrapped up in a purpose that had given us both life and deterioration.

Our remaining show was on the Atlantic coast, near the remains of Coney Island, the first autonomous zone that had been reclaimed from the Regime since their departure from a potentially radioactive Manhattan.

I was ready to lose my shit again, though interspersed with breaks of pining over my bandmate. It was 3 a.m., and we were traversing the at-your-own-risk planks of the Verrazzano and the Goethals bridges to get into town without having to launch the gas-guzzling environmental hyperware of our Astro III that was necessary to enter NYC through the less treacherous Lincoln or Holland tunnels.

The Verrazzano in decay was both a travesty and a work of art, its metallic luster now weathered into green and gold. The Goethals fared about the same. Adjusting to the terrain took guts and wisdom. The shoddy rails were intact yet temperamental enough to scare off any driver who hadn't studied the Bloom's socialist infrastructure. But there was one detail that gave us extra reassurance through it all: the Astra's ability to both hover and float in the event of it taking an unfortunate plunge into the East River.

In darkness, in serenity, we made it across alive. Oracle put on one of my turn-of-the-century favorites. Fulanito burst into song, looked into my eyes, and yelled, "to fruits!"

So, naturally, I responded, "to no absolute!"

"To choice!" Reggy snuck out from beneath the sheets where he'd been hiding from our intoxicated banter for most of the ride.

"To the village voice." Oracle concluded our trifecta of song.

"To any passing fad," Ganache said from a driver's stupor.

"To being an *us.*" Fulanito grabbed my collar, and I nearly fainted, or melted, or some other sinking sensation between a panic attack and arousal.

"Instead of a *them.*" We sang toward one another's faces, and all bets were off. "La Vie Bohème."

We rested, and everyone stared in silence, gawking in the subtle awkward space between awe and annoyance. We were finally home: a sanctuary so bleak that we could not differentiate between joy and exhaustion, as both suffocated and bewildered us alike.

The Astra pulled up to my place. I bid everyone farewell, and to my surprise, Fulanito followed me out the door. And there we were, discarded at the doorstep of my dilapidated flatiron.

My building was Romanesque and ornate, a rare find before Dystopia. Now it was my third arm, my longest appendage, ravaged by weather and riots, and salvaged by a childless thirty-something who had always wanted to be a mother but had instead found apocalypse and a faulty tower begging for care.

Now that the world was in ruins, I could not imagine giving birth as I did in my daydreams. In reality, my kid was made of bricks and concrete, and I now sat at the foot of her altar next to Fulanito. He was pigeon-toed and always recovering from some kind of allergic reaction to nature. As he rolled a joint, I closed my eyes and recalled that tantric breath, that episode, that shameless round of seven minutes in heaven when all we could account for was one another's devoted presence. Still, sexual tension felt unnecessary, almost oppressive amid apocalyptic warfare. We didn't have the time to stare, to stalk, to tiptoe in tandem to one another's insecurities, or to let self-hate lead us into our own demise. We only had time for mistakes and regrets: experimental takes at filling voids. Because I was sick of waking up every day to that numbing routine—jerk off, take a shit, jerk off, pass out, jerk off, max out serotonin, cry a little, fart a little, jerk off, put on my chenille house dress, and make eggs.

I was sick of perpetually asking whether today would be the day I could finally relish in my accomplishments and my home—or at least the day that we would finally kiss. Fulanito twisted the tip of a strawberry-clad joint.

"Here." Fulanito handed me the joint, pressing his lips together to avoid a toothy smile. "You start. I'm shy."

I'm in love with you, I thought to myself as I often did every time he did anything unsuspectingly soft. We looked toward the green and gold strands of fog and gas—the hints of magenta meant it was six o'clock.

There was something about a pink sunset that reminded me why I loved a good cliché. Some things were just timeless—like the electric palate of natural phenomena clashing tirelessly with the threat of industrialization.

"Welp . . . gonna go batten down the hatches." Fulanito stood up with determined glee and extended his arms in an embrace. I held him in return and exhaled.

"It's been so great to see you every day," I said through the fading orange bands of matter that had seen better days.

"Hell yeah." Fulanito squeezed me tighter, and I tried to stop time.

The smokestacks were silent; the cackling drunks and the sneering rats were nesting; the city was truly asleep, and I had forgotten what this calm felt like. In the early morning, there were no longer as many garbage trucks, and there was no longer as much trash, but there was the mysterious smell of aging sea. This was what we called the universal scent of New York spring: decaying gardenias, lost apple orchards, and wilted maple welded into the limestone and, now, a part of the sea.

Every day, I would wake up between the polarizing desire to restore the Bloom or settle into Dystopia. Conviction was obsolete in this world of subtle giants and strategic monsters.

It was early, and I was glowing under the sunrise that crept so slowly behind the yellow, the fog, and the overbearing masterpiece that had become the sky. I looked through the window to the subtle openings in the clouds.

"I'm going to act normal today," I said aloud to myself. "I'm going to splash ice-cold water on my wilting cheek bones, and I'm going to go for a walk. I'm going to sit on hilltops and practice gratitude."

My phone vibrated on my nightstand, and I felt him fourteen blocks away under the Williamsburg bridge in a makeshift balcony on a two-hundred-and-fifty-year-old fire escape that was brave enough to hold the weight of his ferocity. I pulled my phone out to undoubtedly see his name above the blue box and the iridescent cracks in my salvaged magenta gel case.

```
Fulanitx: Hey check out this new song.
```

The song was like a key to his 5th floor apartment, to his fire escape, to the whirlwind tracks between me and his sheltered heart. Our message thread had always been a well of secrets—from the way I spelled his name, our homage to his gender queerness, to the softness of our tone.

We usually exchanged new songs as a .WAV or a .PDF over band dinner or a group email. Then we performed them live so everyone could hear while Oracle and Reggy slowly improvised. Ganache often watched and offered tips. Eventually, we created a song. This was not that, but an open wound, a sacred soliloquy for me to probe, question, and applaud.

Alone on my bed, in my underwear, one hand landed over my palpitating heart while the other held on to my phone, a portal to hell that I usually wanted to destroy but, today, wanted to caress. I stared and gave it time to marinate as it became mine. His new song—on my phone—for me and only me.

I listened to the song without a wink or a sigh and got lost in something that I swore every minute was about me.

CT: wow . . . .*#$% #%$%$ . . . .

I listened to it again, and ten minutes later, I attempted to be professional, as professional artists do.

CT: I don't know what to say . . . it's perfect.

Fulanitx: (✦ ‿ ✦)

Two hours passed in daydreams and in jerking off to the waning sunrise. I couldn't help but question myself: *Was I wise and grounded, or was I a mess and throwing off a schedule that twenty minutes ago was about peace, autonomy, and sitting on a hilltop practicing gratitude but that was now just about Fulanito's song?*

"Carolina, vámanos. ¿No te atragantes el amor antes que te atragantes el poder . . . me oyes, mija?" Ulta would say since she was at peace with my determination to love. Amparo was a bit fearful, but both built a crash pad.

"¡Qué te atragantes el cocimiento y disfruta!" My abuelas persisted.

"¡Y no te olvides de tomar agua, mi amor!" Mamá appeared for maybe the first time. I focused on my heart's wound rather than my rage for the state, and cried for my mother with longing, for the first time since Florida sunk. "¡Dale, mija!"

"¡El cocimiento, la limpia! !" My abuelas ushered me into my truth, and Mamá followed. "¡Atraganta el cocimiento!"

I could not afford another societal crash or emotional trigger getting in the way of my prowess. It was finally time for Forever's gift. I held the velvet bag in my sweaty palms and anticipated feeling the forbidden taboos of practicing self-love in times of collapse.

I turned on Mongo Santamaría and Celia Cruz's Homenaje a los Santos, music that was sacred, and nearly ancient, yet still tortured by the same commercialism that funded the gnarled music industry. I filled my tub with lukewarm water and sang along.

Pulling the red string from the velvet pouch, I revealed the three small amber jars containing Forever's cosimientos—or limpias. The first jar contained a bright floral sludge with the intention of accepting outdated pain, habits, and perspectives that need to be released. The mixture was simple and white with hints of pink and yellow botanicals. I wasn't scared; I was enlightened. I set aside a bowl of cold milk and white roses.

I poured the herbal mixture into the tub's water and then poured the cool milk and white roses over my naked body while I stood above the water. I meditated on my intention to heal wounds and exist beyond the clutches of trauma. I prayed to Yemayá, who facilitaed my righteousness, to Oshun, who held me at my worst, and to Changó, who kept me butch and effortless. I prayed to la Caridad del Cobre and asked that my abuelas continue to carry me and tell me stories, keeping me relevant yet magical. Then I passed out and dreamed of joy. I envisioned simplicity.

"STOP TELLING ME WHAT TO FEEL!" I yelled in my dream into the ether of my long game—into my days of war and nights of sadness that sustained my artistic practice but failed to rebirth me into the world as the artist other people saw. I was used to trailing behind, celebrating my pain, and sitting pretty in my chiffon gowns while I sang about trauma and self-sabotage like a *good* manic pixie, a smart one, a *girlboss,* if you will.

But alas, I got bored of myself. I stopped twirling in my tears and flashing my tits to love myself. It was last year or the year before—I forget—when I started realizing how alone I truly was in a life and in an industry that celebrated gorgeous cesspools of tortured joy where we could turn our trauma into art or kink and then, naturally, be blessed. But my communities had disintegrated since. And as the true fragility of humanity shined with age, our internal chaos and external growth caused bonds to rift, forming individual sects of self-realization.

I missed my nasty punk house full of sad twenty-five-year-old children who transformed the trenches of pain into a colorful circus. Now, however, I accepted the challenge of evolution.

I stood up and exited the bath, draining the water and collecting the botanicals that I would eventually return to the soil. I lay down on the floor surrounded by my records, my journals, and my lifeblood. I stared at the skylight for a time.

I spent the rest of the day floating, resisting my vulnerability, and observing my surroundings. Clarity was as unreal—as calm—as simplicity. So I nurtured an unknown sense of revelation while sitting at the café, minding my time at the riverfront, and basking in the warmth of Fulanito's song without questioning the validity of his heart. Walking home, I smiled and sighed at my reality, sneering at the news and the decay yet hoping for the best.

I woke up ecstatic and replenished, one eye on Fulanito's song and the other on an unknown destination. I walked toward the bathroom and refilled the tub with water in an accelerated pace unknown to the old me. Ruminating to the white noise of the running bath, I brushed my teeth, did a Sun Salutation, and downed a maca frappé concoction with zero added flavor. I opened the jar containing the second cocimiento, the one for releasing trauma.

This jar was composed of something forest green, brown, opaque, wilted, and preserved. I spilled it into the tub and stepped inside. I lay down and rubbed the leaves, the floral hems, and the strange small bulbs all over the parts of mc that carried the most rage, the parts whose foundations were most cracked. I rubbed from the dead ends of my sacrum that loved to remember, to the sweat under my tits that kept me tough and uncomfortable. I laid my body to rest and picked some scabs. I'd never liked to pick my wounds, for they got all over the upholstery. But I picked these scabs because they were loose and unchartered, like home on the road. Then I passed out.

I started to dream about Pluto. I dreamed of beautiful times, like when we'd danced in empty fields and fucked on public transit. I dreamed of Pluto using his proximity to whiteness to steal bath supplies and groceries. I dreamed of Pluto and I telling each other secrets on lonely sheets that did not feel like home. I dreamed of Pluto mocking my pussy.

I dreamed of Pluto waiting on me and Fulanito at a restaurant that was under the sea. We could see dolphins and crustaceans through the windows, and we wanted to order espresso martinis and parmesan-asiago truffle French fries. Pluto was shocked, and I chuckled under my breath.

"That's that one ex . . ."

"The one?" Fulanito gasped while I nodded and smiled, rabid and cynical.

I dreamed of Pluto's father jerking off in his North Bronx living room while Pluto tried to make me dinner in the kitchen. I dreamed of Pluto reminding me to avoid that one hallway so we would not disturb his father. I dreamed of the aimless walks through the three-story brownstone where Pluto had been born and raised, then discarded and mocked as brazen, as queer, as femme, as a genius, as neurodivergent.

I dreamed of Pluto trying to fuck me when I was dry.

I dreamed of Pluto fucking everyone while also fucking them over, because it was always easier for me to save every girl besides myself. I dreamed of how he'd described it to me in shameless, poetic detail.

I dreamed of our dreams, of rock 'n' roll and rolling hills and revolution and creating another world off the grid where we could live in a socialist republic and where he could be a reckless adult teenager and trespass into everyone and everything with zero accountability and where I could be a scene mother, an artist, a matriarch, a vegan chef, and a healer. In the well of deterioration that continued to crack beneath me as long as I stayed pained and reactionary, I dreamed of all the stories I had told and the songs I had written and the quotas I had filled with rage.

I woke up suddenly, gasping for air, and knew that I had realized the dent in my trauma. Revealing the culprit—my brokenness—and a forgotten past, I rested in preparation for the next awakening.

Draining the second bath, I cursed the complexity of forgiveness. I thought of Fulanito and his infectious divinity and the way his pain dwindled into self-righteousness—the lavish kind that inspired me to love myself too. I lay on the shag rug, put on his song, and slept for several hours.

The night was dull, overcast, and gray enough to complement my own destabilization. I woke up to a warm, collective sense of grief and longing. I sat on the window ledge and faced my street, observing the musical synchronicities between my thoughts and the sirens. I stared at my arms covered in bits and fragments of dirt and herbs and clenched my fists, claiming divinity. I rolled a joint and smiled at the city as it dwindled into a moderate midnight blackout.

I grabbed my phone to text my band and reacclimate into civilization but, instead, was greeted by a message from Mercury Lennox—a long-forgotten coconspirator who had always seen my humanity.

Mercury was also Pluto's brother. We'd last spoken in another life, when I'd wanted to be in a band and had not been in a hurry because we'd been thriving and creating culture in a democratic socialist state. Today, Mercury wrote to tell me that he was proud of me. He lamented on an old photo of Pluto and I that he'd found while cleaning up his apartment across the sea in Belarus. A calm yet restrictive plateau between Kyiv and the Kremlin, Belarus had defiantly radicalized since the fall of the Lukashenko dynasty, though it was now being choked by imperialist neighbors.

Mercury's note reminded me of the world, of the global chaos, of the ban on overseas travel and of the decimation of the republic we called home. I fondly remembered the years surrounding 2102 traversing trains, boats, and airplanes wide-eyed and feral and joyfully rallying for revolution. I laughed out loud at Mercury's texted memories of Pluto and I being hilarious and uncouth. I did not give in to my pain but to my glory—I reclaimed my body, and the scathing wounds of Pluto finally crumbled.

I did not think twice, and then I went to bed.

The illusive mysteries of Caribbean Espiritismo were neither rigged nor delusions. Colonization had murdered the divine, but my ancestors held on, crusade after crusade, making sure I could conjure a kind of ungovernable, cosmic healing.

I spent two days resisting my heartstrings and nurturing my actual heart, a muscle and a lifeline toward my own tenacity. I wrote songs, sang to my plants, volunteered at the soup kitchen, made a pie with Reggy, and texted Fulanito no more than I texted Oracle or the super. I bathed away all disbelief and uncovered a pristine, willful girl determined to speak from a place of hope rather than anguish.

A new day rose, and I felt pleasantly numb. I still did not recognize equilibrium, but I'd found it, and I liked it. After my typical routine, I filled the tub with the final installment of bathwater and herbs, hoping for that inspiration to last without my trauma questioning my resurgence or my capacity. I opened the third jar, poured the leafy dark mulch into the bath, and stepped into the scorching tub, the warmest of the three. Closing my eyes, I decompressed, pinching the leaves and regenerated bulbs.

I dreamed of what healing might look like—maybe it would initially feel like another song or a mutual glance from Fulanito. I dreamed further about the complexity of healing and its shape-shifting qualities. One day love was resilience; the next day, it was art; the next, a sunrise; the next, a cup of coffee that reminds you that maybe you already have created another world without the wounds you once called home.

I dreamed of Pluto walking away on a healing path that I was no longer responsible for. He walked toward the embers, the swaying pines, the gravestones we'd skipped over, the secret spots where I'd gone down on him, and our hearts that'd swelled when punk rock had become our savior. He walked onward—between canvas patches, vegan potlucks, and reactionary bliss stitched with dental floss on decaying denim—into his next life, wherever that is now, and away from the memories of us skipping over stones and realizing revolution.

I woke up in a daze, slowly remembering who I was. I accepted that the green chiffon and the extravagant bangs and the unnecessary sequins were only a mask when they stopped being dangerous.

I began weighing the way my art had become my job and how my voice had become my currency even though my heart had stayed human; thus, I was tired. I wanted to rest, so I lay in the slippery mulch. Then I felt a storm, an awakening.

The more I ruminated on Forever's potion, the more I saw a human in Pluto alongside the monster that had been interwoven into once innocent bones and ravaged by the thread of patriarchy. My memories of Pluto became harsh like that of any ex-lover under siege, yet forgiving, like an ancestor.

I dreamed of my family of magicians and curanderas, and I dreamed of my mother calling me three times a day for most of her life to make sure that I was still alive. I dreamed of the birthdays, the holidays, and the revolutions that had made having a family a saving grace. The grieving process had become a means to fight back—never an open wound.

I dreamed of my family protecting us from violent histories of the planet, and I dreamed of my family's idealistic gusto to destroy the Regime in the name of my abuelas.

I rolled sideways in the leaves and the dirt, my eyes spinning toward my brain, shocked at how living in the closet for half my life didn't immediately teach me how to walk away from toxic love with the same revolutionary grace I'd used when I'd broken through societal walls to come out.

Navigating the ruins and resurrections, I found a calm epicenter between passionate urgency and starting over. I ran the shower and stood beneath it, closing my eyes and swallowing the mist.

I was officially human beyond my capacity. I became sick of the prophecies, the fortunes, and the manifesting. Healing should not be this lonely, but it was.

So, I sulked, and I hoped, and I jerked off on the soft cotton sheets that I'd thrown across my bed in an attempt to feel normal, as if I didn't make my bed every day, as if I were unapologetically feral. I dug into my pillows and dreamed about the future—a future of freedom from grieving and of agency found in desire.

CLOSE ENCOUNTERS

Eventually, the future reared its head.

My daily routine had changed. I'd wake up at six and did not have to worry—I only had to remember to breathe regularly. I strategically avoided reminders of the people and places and institutions who had hurt me simply by avoiding things that triggered me—which should have been easy since I was supposed to be incapable of such an emotion. I sprayed Agua de Florida on my temples every few hours so I was not susceptible to pain and vampires. Then I did some kind of mindful movement like walking in nature or dancing to musical theater on abandoned monuments and such.

Long walks mended the disparity, but life happened a little too often, and honestly, I got tired of the universe's daily lessons that forced me to long for Fulanito on a balcony or somewhere closer. So instead,

I'd spend the days making altars and studying intentional movement—not just dancing to punk rock but adapting decolonized systems of healing—like capoeira, transcendental meditation, and aligning my body with ancestral percussion, all of which helped me to shape-shift my scars.

Cheap Glitter's week off was waning, but I did this routine daily in order to smile and feel alive, and it was strange. I wanted to savor these moments of unexpected calm because they were elusive and rare, though I prayed for the day they wouldn't be. However, for now, I basked in the fragility of peace as a livid survivor who was galivanting about the planet without any remorse for anyone who I may have upset because I had felt like a victim once.

The night before our homecoming, I put on my boots and my armor and my black eyeliner and rushed out the door to begin my walk toward the muddy pillars and stacked balcony views of the Pier 17 Resistance Theater for the *#FUCKYOU* show.

My truth, my boundaries, and my desire had been keeping me pretty fucking lonely, but at least I had New York and its gleaming, resilient sparkle—where every lonely night was followed by a new morning in a new place I had never been or by a familiar morning in an old place where I had known a thousand lives.

It was my first night out in old New York since hell knew when and since I was without a task or a performance or a job or a purpose. I could only think of one thing, and so I held my breath as I walked into the amphitheater and waited patiently for the music to start.

I looked for my friends but instead found a solemn corner in the VIP section where I could feel tough, vulnerable, and at peace. Fulanito found me and stood a couple of inches away, crossing his arms and facing the stage lights and a depleted soundboard.

"Hey you!" I stood closer to him. "What's going on?"

"Feelin' pleasantly awkward." Fulanito smiled. "I'm not going to drink tonight."

"Same here. I don't want to get emotional." Fulanito might have thought I was referring to the Regime, but I meant my heart.

"I don't want to do anything I will regret." Fulanito laughed it off.

Suddenly human, I sort of missed being at peace with his unavailability, like when we'd been sequestered into the roving, padded room of a devoted musical relationship or when I'd been just another topless hot girl in his vacuum of disposable internet boners. I missed when flirting had meant nothing because fascism was looming, Florida was sinking, and I did not have the self-awareness to climb to my highest pillar.

But alas, I was now cleansed—*Santísima*—and withering on the edge of reprisal and giving zero fucks. I was now healed from the wounds, the holes, and the debris of victimhood. And so, now I knew the only thing holding me back from speaking my truth to lovers and prospects and the winding unknown was my nascent self-hate.

What the hell had Forever even put in that cocimiento, if not the actual Holy Spirit? Frankly, this power was polarizing, and for now, I feared it.

Understanding the depth of Fulanito's longing was both a gift and curse, and to resist reactionary prowess during an apocalypse was to resist desire and intuition. Resisting the awareness of our colliding hearts when he was somewhere else, however, felt futile regardless of whether he was mending his subconscious, living out his fuckboy fantasies, or uninterested in kissing me in this lifetime.

After so many nights of getting gaslit by my spirit, I felt like a shameful inconvenience, but I no longer had it in me to offer small talk or reactionary cues. I no longer wanted an easier route to the interiors of his heart space, his brain, or his Forty Below sleeping bag that peculiarly rested on porches most nights of tour because *"everything always makes more sense during the sunrise."*

Goddammit, I fucking loved him . . . love and its profound unfamiliarity.

I did not understand this submissive sensation of forgiveness and weakness thriving in a divine context because everything he did was so fucking beautiful—from the way he would ash his joints with one suspended pinky to the way he talked to animals and pressed his lips at a half smile instead of saying yes. Fulanito saw beauty in jagged, asymmetrical aesthetics and ideologies and I, uncharacteristically, learned to do the same as I accepted the polarizing effects of this platonic relationship/romantic friendship—an emotional purgatory. Love was not a switch but a plague coursing through my arteries and my veins.

Staring into the stage lights and the cooling reflections on his hair, I ignored the demons that had caressed our self-denial. Love, a plague so healing, had kept us unencumbered and powerful, and there was no time to be *broken and unavailable* in an apocalypse.

"Why are they starting with my song? I am not ready!" Fulanito ran into the crowd, wailing in fits of ecstasy to that one song I had first heard in fragments while riding shotgun to his erratic playlists of hot and cold and then had heard in full, in isolation, because it was *his* song.

I loved to watch him thrive, and, for once, I danced toward him. Glaring disco-ball reflections spun around the room. The crowd coalesced against the stage, and we became anonymous. We became mortal.

Fulanito looked reckless and aware. We made eye contact and paused. The song continued to the rhythm of the rotating lights, and we remained suspended. Fulanito turned around, dancing in a sublime crevice beneath the elevated speaker that clasped the room in both a daze and a headlock. I took his hand, and he turned to me and smiled, brushing his body against mine and resisting the ambient vibrato. I nuzzled into his armpit, and he rubbed his hand through my hair. I faced up, and my lips could reach his ear.

"This is the song you like" was the line I was going to say, as the floorplan for this very moment had lived in me for months. This song about apricots and being an unhinged woman or an avocado or something—I forget. I just knew that it kept him at peace. In my floorplan, he would smile or say "Fuck yeah," and I would ask to kiss him, or I would just kiss him after I'd brushed my cheek against his soul or whatever force field was keeping him fiercely disgruntled in an ivory tower he had never even asked to be put in.

I stood on my toes to reach closer to his ear, and my boots suppressed their once powerful soles. I slipped, and Fulanito caught me, repositioning us into a waltz or a distressed fit of passion. I caught his eyes knowing I had traveled these electric currents before, though these were the roads less traveled: the cryptic and inflamed bloodshot branches surrounding his ancient light. My complex debris needed his sobering simplicity as his wounded soldier needed my elevated goddess.

We could not help but entwine this way, in this inconvenient, inescapable, effortless way.

Fulanito ran three fingers up my jawline and pulled me toward his. He let out a subtle breath, and I took in a deep sigh of relief, exhaustion, despair, and unexpected arousal.

And then he kissed me.

We kissed beneath the rotating disco ball, its die-cut shards of glass and everlasting glimmers of light. Finally positioned at this climactic intersection, I forgot what I had come to do. I forgot how to speak and how to breathe and how to relate to a world so loveless that it's a balm for the lonely but a minefield for the contented.

Fulanito's lips held mine in a rare tenderness my body had yet to know. I stood taller and swerved my tongue into his, causing a burst of incandescent reflection. Escalating to a warmer embrace, like lost souls or rabid animals, I opened my eyes, looked into his, and exhaled. He stared back with sluggish fuck eyes and kissed me harder.

How was it real? Was mere survival not enough of a gift in this decaying colonized jungle? Imposter syndrome was also real yet almost obsolete in this new and perfect storm. So, I let the storm engulf me.

The reflections of the glass kept us feeling electric. We had not even asked for perfect, and yet we got cosmic.

Maneuvering the subtle notes of healing and destruction, we found tea tree floss and last night's dinner, coastal sand at sunrise, and moss in the spring. Heaven could no longer wait. We inhaled the doubt, the denial, and the vague poetry.

We kissed undercover, under duress, and under a perfect glow that reflected around us every time we stopped to stare and retract the truth that we were actually kissing.

The Two of Hearts as a finale was so cliché during a wholehearted resistance because humanity in Dystopia was not casual and circumstantial—it was drastic and epic and intentional. Under siege, we'd caressed our traumas, our lifeless triggers, and our reactionary cues to fight or flight because how the fuck else could we wake up and blankly *accept* the dim light of New America that had destroyed our oxygen and forced us to be warriors when we really just wanted to play in a rock 'n' roll band or fall in love?

ONLY THE
LONELY

The music stopped. Walking next to him from the venue gates to the Seaport promenade and up to Renwick square, I felt weightless. Then we scurried into my building and tumbled onto the upholstery.

I lay there in Fulanito's arms after maybe the best night of my life according to today's forecast and the subtle glow of my insides.

I rested for hours that felt like eons on Fulanito's sun-stricken skin—smooth and warm and sometimes blotchy from survival. I traced the lines on his face that reminded me of every blessing and every lesson. I followed the rhythmic debris of his deafening laughter, full of conviction, as it moved toward the memory of his crude glances full of elusive heat. Fulanito was the springboard that kept me driven and afloat—and I was his anchor.

As Fulanito and I persisted, I started spending my days doing *normal* things like enjoying a meal, listening to music, and talking to friends about the system and the collapse but also the new hydroponics and their interpersonal realities. I was no longer my trauma.

As warriors, we chose resistance, action, creation, and rule breaking; but as humans facing our greatest demons in generational, societal, and subcultural warfare, we chose rest.

THE GIRL WHO CONQUERED HER DEMONS

During our week off, the news had grown increasingly threatening as our lives became increasingly at peace. This wasn't new, as throughout the tour, the Regime had grown enamored by even more unnecessary growth and by the forbidden contents of our Earth's mantle. The mantle was about 1,800 miles thick, sitting far beneath the Earth's surface. Fawning over the fraught designs of skyscrapers and dense metropolises, New America wanted a new Earth with tunnels and passageways leading to internal BioDomes, and multi-unit structures housing both devout and naive sheep. That summer, the Regime continued its quest for manifest destiny and unnamable threat. Drilling ensued, as did an unnerving new trepidation. Nevertheless, we held down our sanctuaries and our respites, as threat had always been entwined in Dystopian routine.

However, this time was different in both systemic aggression and interpersonal revolution.

We were just another famous rock 'n' roll band trying to coexist in a world that needed a distraction as much as it needed a savior. Playing music and avoiding the pitted trenches of emotional investment had made us tick for long enough, but eventually, I succumbed to my vulnerability and chose painfully arousing submission.

I no longer festered in cyclical purgatory but thrived in a timeless fantasy about being held down on beds of roses to my favorite songs. I could turn off the news and the environmental warfare, and then my fantasy would become the only true story, a fantasy about me getting loved or fucked so hard that my vital life force snapped from fresh survivor to wicked crone in one fell swoop. Fulanito and I no longer needed oxygen. We were oxygen.

Somewhere between the East River and the planked shores of the South Street Seaport, we played an all-ages show. Normalcy was now interwoven between the life I had been fighting for and a life where I could kiss Fulanito in my home, in my dreams, and in public.

Today, we were going to be normal.

"Yeah, let's be normal." Fulanito chuckled while we lined our cheekbones with stars and our wrists with gauze and spikes.

"Fuck yeah, I'm going to be normal—I'm going to wear leggings." I paired my leather accoutrements with casual comforts.

"Fuck yeah, I'm going to wear beige silk." Fulanito tried something new.

"Fuck yeah, fucking poser." I made him laugh, and he kissed me, and we fell onto the floor and stared like we used to.

"Hey, y'all better not make each other pregnant—we have so much to do!" Oracle styled her hair in a glorious, barbed-wire top bun. We all laughed and digressed into a state of *normal*.

That day, Cheap Glitter would skip the pussy-dick-ass banter and celebrate life through the untapped joy of an all-ages space.

I knew of all-ages punk shows catering to generations of angst, but Dystopia was untamed and unlimited. All ages meant a playground of thousands of unlike minds looking for respite. It meant family values against violence, coercion, and growing up too fast, as violent systems often thrust people into a post-traumatic wisdom we did not ask for.

The matinee show was filled with kids: kids painting faces, kids playing pin the tail on the horses and mules, kids yelling and screaming and asking us why we looked like this—asking questions like, Why do we have tattoos if they hurt? Why do we play music? Why do we not seem scared as the environment crumbles beneath the shallow rule of empire?

We did not know how to tell them, so we showed them why they were worth our labor, the drudgery, and the danger. We played every song for free, for hours, facing one of those skies we always looked forward to—a sky with maybe less methane and more antioxidants. These sunsets were monolithic, a symbiosis between people and nature in the face of destruction.

At dusk, nearly five thousand comrades, enemies, kids, and their parents jumped up and down below the Brooklyn Bridge during a rare moment of collective hope. Dystopia was a calm flame and a glorified playground, as it always had been. Tour felt distant, our efforts felt needed, and as a band, we were full.

The show was over, and we partied as we had hundreds of times

ABOLITION NOW
HISTORY OF THE WORLD
FREE PEOPLE'S MARKET
VIVA LA REVOLUCION!

before, assured of the demons we'd slayed. I tried to hang on to the surprising peace that came from the thousands of kids screaming in our honor as I walked toward home, clasping my gear and Fulanito's arm. Oracle followed us with a backpack of sticks and cables hinged to her shoulders while she smiled at the sky behind a sequined bandana that covered her mouth. Reggy and Ganache trailed three feet behind, cackling in hysteria over some new memory—a testament to hope.

"Hey, wanna hang out later?" Fulanito draped his saxophone over his right arm and inched toward my ear.

"Yeah, I wanna hang out." I laughed and cowered into my shirt collar. Fulanito growled and bit my cheekbone. "But I have to go pickup pantyliners and ibuprofen on the way."

Fulanito pointed west to show me something that was not there and kissed me from the east as I looked away. I looked back toward the east, and our mouths locked for a few seconds that would eventually last forever in my mind.

I stopped at a public mall to cleanse my sacral void. Fulanito lingered, and the security guard led me to a bathroom in the back.

"Nice ink," the guard said, pointing to his chest, suggesting he was looking at mine, where *traviesa* was tattooed in black script. As I was closing the stall's door, I saw his feet shuffle less than two inches from the stall, so I let the marching band in my asshole serenade the storage room as it would a parade, much to the dismay of his boner's expectations. I sat there and stewed in the doldrums of horny men and public restrooms and my own reactionary responses to humanity's collective loneliness. I took in the sterile scents of cardboard and nylon and waited for something to remind me that I hadn't lost my mind, that happiness was a birthright. I flushed amid a forceful echo.

"Good night, sir!" I exited the restroom. The security guard saluted me, and I scrambled toward Fulanito. I was now teetering on the edge of that dangerous love that made me less afraid of dying, that dangerous love that debilitated my sense of time and space—a sense that was both a resource and a gift. I was hanging onto the limbs of that dangerous love that makes you forget and amplify your purpose all at once.

We reached the Coney Island boardwalk at dusk. The crumbling circus had been reborn with every revamp, so here, we found normalcy. We walked and laughed, enthralled in a sensory overload where my feet did not touch the ground and my body was wholly integrated in all aspects of the space we inhabited. Embodiment was a strange animal to the survivor of trauma, as it began with acknowledging that we even had a body.

I didn't yet *get* this elation, this love, this freedom, this sense of self that thrived on a near holy plane. Joy in this world was a diamond in an eternal rough, and I was shocked to have found it. We shuffled toward the sea on the decaying planks that had been destroyed by our worst enemies and preserved by us. We carried on, and together we wondered what it would feel like to lose New York—to die and live among the ghosts of whales and skyscrapers, oligarchs, and heroes.

We kissed and tumbled to the ground, and my back rested on the warm golden-hour sand. Crystal granules found refuge in each one of our crevices while we kissed and fucked and occasionally gasped for air.

The sky looked ominous and livid with black clouds and cracks of magenta, a sight as horrifying and as beautiful as every memory that had brought us here. I thought of the waves ushering in the first time I had caught Fulanito following me along the shore of the Riis channel—before waves were threats and air was poison. I'd been lying alone in sweat and sand, my tits burning first and my heart burning last, and I'd watched him inch toward me on a shitty surfboard; we were seconds away from our first deep conversation about life and opera and mortality.

TOTAL

That was the day I'd learned Fulanito's astrological chart was earth-dominant. As a water-dominant person, I'd learned we were meant to meet halfway on the shore to create respite from the chaos of fire, of air, and of never knowing ourselves beyond our own suffering.

Inside, I'd known that we were meant to exist in an eternal state of revelry. I'd known we were meant to speak in coded tongues twisting on highways that traversed the best nights of our lives.

When I saw him on the beach that day, I thought it would be the first time we'd kiss; today, I wondered whether it would be the last.

For the first time, I believed in love and in his word, and I only feared the futility of Dystopia.

Nestled in communion and the infinite tug-of-war between fearing for my life and kissing Fulanito, I now knew love would only stand still when I was ready to fall.

"We gotta believe in the power of our debris . . . not just the songs . . . but the energetic shit we leave behind." Fulanito sparked a joint while we sat on what had become our spot on the 37th Street side of the Coney Island shore. We were wrapped in a blanket, glowing from orgasms and hollow with exhaustion. "It's, like, the only way to die."

The rain came down, and we piled into the Astra and told more stories. We sneered at and mocked our past selves, staring into one another and imagining revolutions and future generations thriving without empire, without insurgency, but with stars and eternity, as we had once known.

Fulanito drove us back onto the mainland. I asked for a night apart for reflection, and he obliged. We turned on the radio to despairing podcasts riddled in anxiety and doomed prophecies. I changed the station to the 2099 classics—the oldies radio. We drove into the city triumphant, grounded. Reaching my stop, I turned toward the door to unlock it, and he pulled me toward him and kissed me again. I stumbled toward the street with my eyes on his.

"See ya later," I said to him as I smiled without restraint.

Walking through town, taking notes in journals, and planning revolutions, I was now living as I never had before.

I could finally be a true warrior, I thought as I smiled at stars and scoffed at the Regime's imperial blimps that would often visit to spread propaganda.

I planned a future that looked like the past, I thought to myself. *Except this time, I would not be drunk, or broken, or hinged on the prospect of love. I would be free because I was finally divine.*

I walked down an alleyway and saw the dripping black writing on a dimly lit concrete wall:

"I THINK I'LL HATE MYSELF TONIGHT, AND I DON'T CARE! BECAUSE TOMORROW I'LL BE OVER YOU! SO RIGHTEOUS, SO SELF-AWARE! TONIGHT'S FOR OPEN WOUNDS, TIRED LUNGS, AND A SENSE OF DOOM . . . TOMORROW, I'LL BE OVER YOU."

Little hearts were scribbled below the text next to an assorted array of musings ranging from "Giovanni4eva," "I LOVE GioVANNI," "Giovanni ISBOO" to "Fuck the Regime" and "DIE AI." This was new—to see my words so large and so inflated and more powerful than I had ever seen myself in this body full of haphazard history. My vision realigned with this new consciousness. This was no longer my story; it was someone else's, and it was perfect.

I had never seen myself through the lens of the kids, whose power shined beyond my own when we screamed together at any given night. To have loved me then, in my drunk shambles and all, may have just been the divine love I'd sought for so long.

I sat down and stared without shame or self-deprecation but overdue admiration for the girl who'd conquered her demons with glitter and grace.

SEPTEMBER 2121

I woke up to another earthquake, to another shattered glass petri dish that I'd forgotten to Velcro to the tallest altar. I made myself my latte: cardamom, fennel, and rare earth swirling in a whirlpool of frothy oat milk and cinnamon. The cardamom and fennel secured my gut microbiome, and the rare earth came in the form of motherwort, lemon balm leaf, black cohosh, and the profound scent of Fulanito's embrace. The placebo effect sustained me on these dismal days of living fast.

"Hey! Can I come over?" I called Fulanito on this particularly musky Monday morning.

"Please?" Fulanito concurred. I put on slip-ons and a T-shirt that had seen better days and prepared—in my head—for the best night of my life.

I had lived my life creating things that could hopefully make the world stronger. I had watched the resistance turn our dollars into longevity by vetoing societal threats and reclaiming land. The essence of failure now felt outdated, because as long as society was so beyond atrocity, our notion of success would seldom abide by their standards. Now, whatever we did for survival was inherently breathtaking.

I repeatedly reinvented self-preservation because depression was annoying when the world watched you succeed and romanticized the illusion of your suspiciously lonely yet charmed life. Still, hope felt stupid sometimes—as if I were there, waiting for a revolution that would dismantle the state but might just only exist inside my soul.

REDEMPTION SONG

Later that September, the internet was flooded with headlines on mass deportation, potential mass executions, and a movement presented by the Regime called Democratic Elimination, the state's justification of ethnic and social cleansing via abduction and mass murder. The bulk of this violence was posed as a preliminary to end-stage capitalism, where populations unwilling to bargain were eliminated to allow artificial intelligence and the oligarchical elite to set in motion initiatives that could possibly destroy humanity. Such initiatives included oceanic industrialization, the development of Earth's mantle, and the globalization of New America. But despite missionaries, digital brainwashing, and ecological trespassing into our private Dystopias, we remained dangerously protected by truth, love, song, and coalitions against imperialism.

New America was, in theory, anti-war but enjoyed threatening us with it if we did not behave. Because the Bloom had begged for peace through socialist policies and because we still revered self-sufficiency over artillery, ecological warfare felt like a weapon we could only fight through the belief that something larger than us would eventually come.

OCTOBER 2121

We woke up to no internet.

It wasn't a faulty connection but an intentional destruction of all global networks in order to block the exchange of knowledge while the Regime engaged in environmental terrorism.

Suddenly, we were all we had.

Dystopia thrived through community, song, dance, and a prayer for a universe that honored humanity before capital gain. Dystopians believed that somewhere, someday, some distant land or planet would be able to hold space for trees, for animals, for people, and for reclamation of the spirit.

We were wounded soldiers but evolved enough to love. Evolution felt like seeing beyond the games, the manipulations, and the insecurities of those you loved as their intent sprawled before you like a glorious elephant in a perfectly sized room. Now we could love unconditionally by breathing wildly and navigating one another's imperfections with humility.

We were exhausted from having spent our twenties and thirties being all too broken to see ourselves. We owed it to one another to be tender and forgiving as we effortlessly caroused around town. As reactionary self-proclaimed degenerates with zero filter, it was suddenly necessary to step back and prioritize vulnerability.

Maybe the greatest love story ever told wasn't about finding *the one* but about finding your way home.

We spent these days performing and praying and dismantling whatever progress the Regime had enacted on us whether through direct action or solemn intention.

Reggy was the caretaker of a thriving hydroponic forest, a living room he had dreamed of since his forests had been forsaken. Oracle learned hitchhiking on hoverships from Gemmx, and soon, traversing between Montreal and New York became easy, as the burgeoning culture between our cities had led to side projects and the stark fullness of Oracle's heart. Ganache was skateboarding and thrashing and living a rendition of a best life that inspired us to nurture peace.

Fulanito and I forged rituals and wrote songs. We began meeting halfway on the Williamsburg bridge for sunsets, stray dolphins, stray spacecraft, stars, and strands of light pollution as if it were a religious procession. The sanctity of our peace was unlike any accolade or any moment of effective notoriety. Fulanito taught me how to evade fear and despair, and I rested in the knowledge that I had found everything I had been looking for.

NOVEMBER 2121

There were no headlines—just an intuitive acceptance of what was to come based on the view from our homes and sanctuaries.

Tectonic plates are large slabs of rock that make up Earth's crust. They shift constantly and reshape the earth's landscape in tune to an ancient, untapped rhythm. This rhythm had been composed by intergalactic gods and warriors, Neolithic organisms, and a fierce conductor just shy of mad genius—the Earth itself. If this rhythm is disrupted, the plates resist with no remorse, causing earthquakes, tsunamis, and a plethora of other reactionary trauma responses.

DECEMBER 21ST 2121

The day was for respite, resistance—anything but the news—so I hosted a brunch.

Later that afternoon, a 9.2 magnitude earthquake throttled East Dystopia, causing massive floods and unexpected mine explosions.

This was not a natural disaster but a reaction against six hundred years of imperialism. It was the Earth in chains, lashing out because it could no longer resist the systemic torture.

Cheap Glitter sat in my living room with acoustic guitars and bottles of home brew in hand while dim candles lit our greatest achievements hanging on the pastel pink walls of the sanctuary I called home. We could not face the truth, so we faced each other with the adamant recollection of a job well done and the belief that this will surely awaken some kid somewhere in a distant future. We sang along to our favorite songs, Amparo's songs, Ulta's songs, and "Total Waste"—Fulanito's opus and our catalyst.

Outside, the elements raged, and the concrete unfurled. As the ground sliced itself apart, the ocean crashed in tandem.

Cheap Glitter

Our home was destroyed. Every living, breathing organism in East Dystopia was disrupted and engulfed.

We swore our revolution was eternal. Alas, we were just mortal rabble-rousers and the seeds they could not poison, so we'd sown ourselves into feral beasts and great healers.

The earth was now igniting a global revolution against environmental destruction, urging a regeneration of humanity. The earth was both a killer and a beacon, a class war and a lesson. It fought off its worst enemies and grieved its greatest devotees, hoping for a semblance of a future in the places the Regime had not yet harmed.

In West Dystopia, communities huddled en masse, overlooking the Pacific with keepsakes and rage intact. West Dystopians knew the cycles of the planet as well as they knew breath and compassion. As wildfires and earthquakes equally ravaged the once fertile world, the people became the land: a symbiotic catalyst that the West knew too well, albeit never like this. The land enveloped our sanctuaries and signaled east.

In tandem, the East rippled toward the center. The Dystopias met in a radiant collision, an ecstatic waltz. Transmuting a thousand years of masterworks and paragons into a weapon of mass destruction, the cracks swelled, and New America was detrimentally consumed.

In a cadence of divine intervention, the BioDome cracked, and the decaying concrete beneath could no longer suffice.

The Regime was finally destroyed.

Cheap Glitter tumbled into the sea and into the crevices of New America's *New Earth*. New America was now a ruin, a land mine, a gas leak on the edge of civilization.

We stopped breathing.

Our bodies, now land, traversed the new Earth as eternal footprints that told stories of love and resistance. Our safe havens were now shrines, sacred artifacts and buried treasure. However, Cheap Glitter would live forever in countercultures, in social movements, and in the self-evident impact of the trajectory of rock 'n' roll.

As humanity mourned in solidarity, Cheap Glitter's message became universal, and our songs survived as both armor and reprieve for the rest of the world. After all, what was the value of fame without a profound imprint on humanity? Cheap Glitter was an imprint that forged a transcontinental ripple effect— a universal language of revolution.

This procession was not our ride, our scenic view, or our comforting song to fall asleep to; it was monuments falling in simultaneous thunder and the raw, unprecedented accountability of the state. It was the consecration of our legacies embossed into history and relics. It was the resurrection of insurrections to come and the longed-for demise of American imperialism.

It wasn't the end of the world, but the end of a world power that had offered violent reform and rampant corruption to a people who had begged for a compassionate revolution.

It was the end of Dystopia, and the end of *our* world—where we'd thrived against giants and turned cheap glitter into gold.

THE END

ACKNOWLEDGMENTS

Thank you to Mamá, to my tias, my sister, my primos, and my abuela for keeping me alive, for loving me and feeding me and taking me seriously whether I was writing a romance novel or a fanzine. Thank you for inspiring me to do the same for them. Thank you to my family who has apologized for the chaos, giving me strength and wisdom. Thank you everyone who played in or collaborated with The Homewreckers or Choked Up, traveled the world, slept in garbage, cried during band meetings, celebrated our rage, and ate Arby's or raw fruit three times a day—only to lose sleep or get sick, all for the sake of playing our songs. Thank you for carving space for my trauma, my Saturn Return, my pushing forty, and my awakenings while trusting me with your own. Thank you to my co-conspirators and chosen family who let me tell the same stories over and over. Thank you to the art scenes, activist circles, and best friends that were born out of a need to resist and create another world. Thank you for inspiring theses characters and the moments that make this story. Thank you to Michelle Tea for being a healer and a mentor, for taking *Sink or Burn* on tour twice and believing in the right for this story to exist. Thank you to everyone who read through this book and edited, cried along, and convinced me to keep going: J Oberman, Ileana Vila, Avi Ehrlich, Angelica Sgourous, Amy Scholder, Ever Velasquez, Nicole Georges, Mariah Stovall, James Spooner, and Nate Powell. Thank you to my extraordinary team at Row House press: V. Ruiz, Rebekah Borucki, Lisa Bond, and Meghan Rollins—thank you for believing in a story that seemed to terrify the rest of the world. Thank you to every collaborator and coconspirator who has educated me on what it truly looks like to be on the right side of history, to everyone who read my fanzine once in 1998 but continues to send me postcards or put me on the guest list for every show. Thank you to my muses, my exes, and my great love who taught me the value of fighting and crying and acting unhinged to eventually rise above our worst selves. Thank you for showing me how to write a love story.

Thank you, Chippy, for teaching me patience and unconditional love.

ABOUT THE AUTHOR

Eternal rabble-rouser, Cristy Road Carrera is a first-generation Cuban-American artist, writer, and musician. Blending anti-fascist principles with survival love stories, Carrera has spent over twenty-five years testifying to the beauty of the imperfect.

Her career began in 1996 with a self-published punk rock fanzine that sparked decades of illustrating for music, literature, and social movements. After forging an imprint in queer, feminist countercultures with graphic memoirs, illustrated novels, and punk rock records, Carrera redefined her career in 2019 after writing, illustrating, and releasing the *Next World Tarot*, a seventy-eight-card deck that envisions a world based on radical redefinitions of self-love and social justice.

Carrera is a singer and songwriter and has been fronting punk rock bands since her days of self-publishing fanzines. She currently performs her songs in the band Choked Up, making records and playing shows with the ancient punk rock ethos of passion before profit. Engaging with her world in spaces ranging from Yale University to Bluestockings Bookstore, Cristy Road Carrera continues to thrive on the fringe of the mainstream and in the epicenter of revolution.